Kindred Blessings

Elizabeth Penney

Annie's®

AnniesFiction.com

Books in The Inn at Magnolia Harbor series

Library of Congress-in-Publication Data
Kindred Blessings / by Elizabeth Penney
p. cm.
I. Title
                        2019948256

AnniesFiction.com
(800) 282-6643
The Inn at Magnolia Harbor™
Series Creator: Shari Lohner
Editor: Lorie Jones
Cover Illustrator: Bonnie Leick

10 11 12 13 14 | Printed in China | 9 8 7 6 5 4 3 2 1

Amy

This can't be happening.

Amy Prescott Butler clutched her husband's arm. The fine gray wool suit was so unlike Abel, who lived in polo shirts and jeans, even in his position as vice president of a booming Atlanta tech company. But he'd insisted, saying a suit was appropriate for the occasion.

The occasion. Amy bit her lip, fighting back a wave of dizzy disbelief. She couldn't believe they were seated in an attorney's office in northern Georgia, waiting to hear the contents of her grandmother's will. Amy hadn't even known her grandmother was sick, although she'd been well over eighty and death could have called anytime.

A chill ran over her, making her shiver under her blazer. Just yesterday they'd gotten the call, a bald announcement of Dorothy Prescott's death and an appointment to meet with her attorney. Her grandmother hadn't wanted a funeral service or even a family gathering.

A short, spry man with gray hair entered the office.

Abel stood up, dragging Amy with him.

"Good morning," the man said, approaching them with his hand extended. "You must be the Butlers. I'm Phillip Watson, your grandmother's attorney." He shook their hands with a firm, dry palm, his lively eyes regarding them with interest. "I'm sorry for your loss."

"Thank you," Amy said.

Phillip gestured for them to be seated again and hurried around to take his place at the desk. He sat down, pulling the rolling chair closer to the desktop. "Your grandmother and I go way back. After we both retired up here, we stayed in touch. Wonderful woman."

"You're retired?" Abel asked, his voice a low yet authoritative rumble. He was tall and lean, with a calm demeanor, so the force of his personality once he exerted it was often a surprise. Amy enjoyed watching people reassess their opinions of her husband.

The attorney cocked his head and studied Abel. "Not entirely, as you can see. I kept my practice open for several valued clients. Your grandmother was one."

Since Dorothy Prescott had been an extremely wealthy woman with property all over Atlanta, Amy was sure Phillip had been loath to part with her lucrative business. Amy's belly hollowed at the realization that the estate now belonged to Amy and her siblings, her grandmother's only relatives.

Not that Amy and Abel couldn't use the money. They were underwater on their house, so they couldn't sell it and buy something more modest. The prices of homes in Atlanta were ridiculous, especially in the historic neighborhood she'd fallen in love with. Most people she worked with commuted into the city, which meant a horrible daily drive in some of the country's worst traffic. Right now, both she and Abel could get to work in fifteen minutes, twenty if traffic was bad. Surely that was worth a lot in the long run.

"We're waiting for your brother and sister to arrive, Mrs. Butler," Phillip said, picking up several folders and tapping them into place. "Then we'll get started."

"Amy," she corrected, although appreciating the older man's courtesy. No one called her Mrs. Butler.

"Would you like coffee?" Phillip offered. "Or bottled water?"

Amy exchanged glances with Abel. The pair practically lived on coffee. "A cup of coffee would be great," she said, suppressing a yawn.

"We were up early." And she hadn't slept at all the previous night, tangled up with shock and grief over the news.

"I'll take a cup too," Abel said. He reached for her hand and squeezed it. "Hanging in there?"

Amy nodded.

Phillip pushed a button on his desk phone and spoke into the intercom. "A tray will be right in," he told the couple.

An uneasy silence fell over the office, uneasy on Amy's part anyway. To calm her jangled nerves, she tried to focus on the view of the mountains through the windows. In the back of her mind, behind the grief and confusion, the awareness of missed work deadlines and tasks loomed. They didn't go away because she had a family emergency. No, her to-do list never shortened. It always nagged her like a low-grade mental virus.

Despite her company's stated commitment to helping employees with self-care, good diet, and exercise, the fact was, working there was only a step up from indentured servitude. They owned her. And Abel's company owned him. But that was the price they paid for being among Atlanta's new elite.

The receptionist entered the room carrying a tray, which she set on the sideboard. "I've got coffee with the fixings," she said, her voice a soft drawl. She fussed with things on the tray, then turned to Phillip. "The other two parties have arrived. They're in the parking lot."

"Good," Phillip said as he rose from his chair.

"I'll show them in," the woman said, then left the room.

Phillip gestured toward the coffee tray. "Please help yourselves."

Amy got out of the chair and tottered across the thick rug, unaccustomed to the high heels she was wearing. Like Abel, she normally wore casual attire. She poured two cups from the carafe and added a splash of non-dairy creamer to each, then handed one to Abel. They took their coffee the exact same way, one of the quirky details that she felt displayed their compatibility.

Standing nearby, Abel took the cup with thanks.

Voices sounded in the foyer, and a moment later, her younger brother and sister appeared in the doorway, escorted in by the receptionist.

Dylan entered first with his usual swagger. He wore an open-collared white shirt with dress slacks and expensive Italian leather loafers. Dylan had the Prescott chin, square and dimpled, as did Amy, although thankfully hers was more feminine. He also had the same strong cheekbones, dark hair, and blue eyes. Dylan was an architect by day and a serial dater by night. Amy loved her brother, but she didn't respect his lifestyle.

Amy had fond memories of Savannah as a sweet little girl who liked to cuddle with her, especially after their parents died in a plane crash. But now, studying the striking young woman in a trendy outfit with her long, highlighted hair hanging to her waist, she had trouble remembering that innocence.

Savannah strode into the room. "What's going on here? Is it true that Grammie is dead?" Her tone was strident, but Amy's heart squeezed when she glimpsed raw fear in her sister's eyes.

Amy jumped up and hurried to her sister's side, attempting to put an arm around her.

But Savannah shrugged her off. "I'm okay," she said, pulling away with a glare. "Let's get this over with. I have to get back to Atlanta."

Savannah worked in fashion as an influencer, meaning she got companies to pay her to post pictures of herself wearing or using their products online. Only in the digital age would such a nebulous, frivolous career be possible. Amy wished that her sister would buckle down and apply her college degree in graphic design and marketing. She had true talent.

Phillip introduced himself to the newcomers, offered them coffee, then ushered them to their seats. Once they were settled, the attorney sat down again. "All right, everyone. We'll get started now."

Something in the man's expression made Amy feel uneasy. She braced herself.

"Your grandmother was an unusual woman," Phillip said. "She was not only a savvy businesswoman who took her inheritance and tripled it—"

Dylan exclaimed softly.

Phillip furrowed his brows. "But she was a philanthropist who supported many charities and her church. She—"

"Don't tell me she left it all to charity." Dylan scowled. "That wouldn't be fair. We were her only relatives. Our dad was her only child."

Phillip raised a hand for silence. "Yes, she did leave money to charity and the church, but the vast bulk of her estate will be going to you three." He paused. "Assuming certain conditions are met."

Amy wondered what he meant by that. The unease she'd felt a moment earlier grew into consternation. She'd begun counting on Grammie's estate to help her and Abel over the hump, and surely it was her due.

Phillip extracted three envelopes from a folder. "Your grandmother had a last request. She wanted you three—and Abel, of course—to spend several days at an inn in South Carolina."

There was an outbreak of questions.

Again, Phillip held up a hand. "Please let me explain. Everything will be made clear. While at the inn, you will have assignments to complete. If you perform them properly, the inheritance will be yours." He passed out the envelopes. "These are notes from your grandmother."

Amy studied the envelope. All it said was her name, scrawled in Grammie's distinctive handwriting. Her insides churned at the idea of reading it, since she hadn't been the best granddaughter. And the challenge was sure to be daunting as well. Grammie hadn't suffered fools gladly, looking down her regal nose at those who couldn't—or wouldn't—excel.

"Who's supposed to determine if we perform our assignments properly?" Dylan demanded, an edge to his voice. "And why should we work for what is already ours?" He slumped back, folding his arms across his chest. "The whole thing sounds ridiculous."

Amy winced at his harsh, rude tone, but she didn't object. He was expressing their thoughts, even though he didn't employ the tact and grace she would have used.

Phillip appeared unruffled. "Your grandmother warned me that you would object to the terms, but she was insistent." His tone was steely. "And it was her money. That's the law, folks. As for who will be monitoring you, she asked me to do it. I'll be staying at the inn too."

After a moment of thick silence, Savannah said with a huff, "Well, let's get it over with. What do I have to do?"

"I'm glad you asked, young lady." Phillip smiled. "You're going to work on an organic farm. As a farmhand."

Savannah gasped.

Before she could object, Phillip turned to Dylan. "And you are volunteering on a project to build a new home for a needy family."

Dylan shifted around in his seat, but thankfully he kept quiet.

"Amy and Abel, you are basically to give up your cell phones for a week, spend time together, and take pottery lessons."

"You two got off easy," Dylan muttered.

Savannah clutched her pink phone, eyes wide.

Amy was stunned by the idea of giving up her phone, but she didn't understand the pottery part. Then she remembered. The family fortune had begun way back in the 1700s with a pottery factory in South Carolina. Grammie had always nattered on about that, and supporting local pottery artisans had been one of her crusades.

"Is the inn anywhere near Magnolia Harbor?" Amy asked. She recalled Grammie mentioning that town.

Phillip nodded. "In fact, you'll be staying at the Magnolia Harbor Inn. It's a lovely antebellum mansion on Lake Haven—"

"Enough with the travelogue," Dylan interrupted. "When does this ordeal begin?"

"Today," Phillip answered. "You'll have time to go home and pack, and then we'll expect you at the inn this evening. It's only an hour north of Charleston so you shouldn't have a problem getting there on time."

Amy glanced at her husband. That meant asking for leave at work, which wasn't an issue since it fell under bereavement. But she hadn't planned to take off so much time due to the project deadlines she faced as a product developer for a tech company, though not the same one Abel worked for. Her department generated new ideas, picked the best ones, and brought them to market. They had several launches coming up. How was she supposed to do this?

"Do we have to go?" her husband whispered, echoing her thoughts. "I really can't afford the time off."

"Me neither," she whispered back. "But we're talking big numbers. Like, um, millions. Many millions."

If all went well, they wouldn't need their jobs. Perhaps they could start their own company that valued people's contributions and didn't treat them like slaves. And maybe, just maybe—she couldn't allow herself to even think the words—but visions of pink and blue bootees danced in her head.

Abel pressed his lips together before finally nodding. It was clear that he didn't like the idea but he'd do it.

Amy squeezed his hand in response. "We're on board. Abel and I will go to the inn." If they'd be able to meet the requirements of the challenge was another story. But she had to give it a try.

Even if she didn't know which task of the three would be the most difficult.

Grace

The October afternoon sky was so deep and blue it made Grace Porter's heart ache.

Careful not to jostle her cargo of pumpkins and potted mums, Grace navigated her Honda CR-V along Lake Haven Road, taking in the sweet signs of autumn. The maple next to Julep Buckley's house had flamed red, and berries hung heavy on the viburnum bushes. Pumpkins lined the porch steps, and clusters of cornstalks adorned a split rail fence.

Perhaps best of all, the air was cool, almost crisp, carrying a hint of burning leaves. This time of year, Grace drove with the windows down, a cozy sweater warding off the breeze.

The stone pillars marking the inn driveway appeared, and she slowed to turn in. Even after years of co-owning the property, she still felt a thrill whenever she returned home.

The 1816 antebellum mansion with its two-story veranda sat nestled among shade trees and gardens, beckoning visitors with a welcoming air. A group of guests was filling most of the inn's rooms later. From what she'd gathered from Phillip Watson, the attorney who had made the reservation, they were staying for several days as conditions of a will.

That was perhaps one of the most unusual reasons for a booking Grace had ever experienced. Most people stayed at the inn for Magnolia Harbor's special events, a family occasion, or simply to relax.

Grace parked in front of the steps and got out to open the rear hatch.

The front door opened, and Winnie Bennett, her aunt, let out Winston, Grace's shih tzu mix. Winnie was the younger sister of Grace's late mother, Hazel Wylde.

Winston gave a happy bark and raced toward her, his little legs churning.

"Glad to see me?" Grace picked up the small dog, laughing when he licked her nose. "You'd think I'd been gone for days, not an hour."

Winnie smiled fondly at the inn mascot. "He kept staring at the door, waiting for you." She lifted a container of mums from the rear compartment. "I love these dark red ones."

"Me too." Grace set the dog down and reached for a bucket. "They'll look gorgeous with the white pumpkins I bought." Small, medium, and large pumpkins were riding in the back seat.

Winnie raised her brows. "I remember the days when you could only get orange."

"Now they've even developed pink and blue ones," Grace replied.

"Imagine that," Winnie said as she placed the mums on the veranda steps.

The front door opened again, this time revealing Charlotte Wylde, Grace's younger sister and co-owner of the bed-and-breakfast. Charlotte, a trained chef and a best-selling cookbook author, was in charge of the inn's scrumptious meals. She waved a manila envelope. "Grace, did you read the instructions for the new guests?"

Winnie put a hand to her mouth. "Oh yes, I meant to mention that. It was delivered by courier a little while ago."

"I haven't seen it," Grace said, setting down another container of mums. She'd bought six. Now it was time to arrange the pumpkins. "What does it say?"

Charlotte perched on a step and removed several pages from

the envelope. "Well, there are dietary requirements," she said, leafing through the papers. "I'll get to those in a minute."

Usually the inn served only breakfast and appetizers during early evening wine and cheese socials. But for the Prescott family, they were going to serve some lunches and dinners as well.

"Here we go," Charlotte said. "Each of the Prescott children—they're all adults—have special projects while they're here."

Grace opened the Honda's back door and pulled out a pumpkin. "Okay. Why do we need to know about it?" Being an innkeeper meant a skillful balance of listening and offering information upon request without being nosy. Many guests at the inn participated in outdoor sports or artistic and cultural pursuits during their visit.

"'I'm requesting your cooperation in helping the heirs successfully meet their challenges during their stay,'" Charlotte read aloud. "'That means not letting them run away from their obligations, assign them to someone else, or bribe anyone to help.'"

"Oh my." Grace set the pumpkin down, then plopped onto the step beside it. "That sounds ominous."

Winnie grabbed two tiny pumpkins from the SUV and brought them over. "I'll say. What did the will ask them to do?" As their right-hand woman, Winnie was privy to almost everything that happened at the inn.

Charlotte exhaled a gust of air with a sigh. "Let's see. Dylan is to help with the Halstead house, Savannah is to work on Roy Bevins's farm, and Amy is to take pottery lessons."

Grace knew about the Halstead project, the construction of a new home for a family whose house had burned down, because it was a community-wide project and she was on the committee. She also knew Roy Bevins. His small organic farm was one of the best in the area, and they often bought his produce and dairy products for the inn. But she was confused about the pottery lessons. Unless . . .

"Do the lessons have something to do with the pottery festival?" Grace asked. The annual festival was this week, and it included demonstrations, a pottery fair, and social gatherings.

"Bingo," Charlotte said. "The late Dorothy Prescott was one of the primary sponsors of the pottery festival. Her ancestors founded Prescott Pottery back in the 1700s."

"That's right." Winnie set down several medium pumpkins, then arranged them next to the mums. "You can still see the ruins of the factory in the woods near the clay pits. It went out of business around 1800." She sat on the step beside Grace. "So our guests have a lineage related to Magnolia Harbor. It's starting to make sense why they're coming here."

Charlotte snorted. "Now that it's settled, hopefully I'll be able to figure out the menus." She held up a piece of paper and jabbed a finger at it. "Amy, who is the eldest, and Abel, her husband, are vegan. Dylan is on the Paleo diet, and the youngest, Savannah, has to be gluten-free. I'll need a spreadsheet to keep track."

Grace sent her sister a teasing smile. "What are you making tonight?" Although it wasn't exactly clear when the guests would arrive due to their travel time, the agreement included this evening's dinner.

Squinting at the instructions, Charlotte ran a hand through her hair. After a moment, she nodded. "A buffet. They can pick and choose whatever they want. As for tomorrow, I'd better put my thinking cap on."

The sound of a powerful engine drifted from the road, drawing the attention of the three women and the dog. The rumble grew louder, then lowered to a purr as a yellow sports car slowed and turned into the driveway.

"That must be one of them now," Winnie said. "I don't recognize the car."

Charlotte barked out a laugh. "Three guesses. I'll bet it's Dylan."

As though mesmerized, they sat and watched the low-slung vehicle make its way down the drive, passing the guest parking area and continuing onto the half-circle drive that led to the front door. A moment later, the car stopped and the door on the driver's side swung open.

A handsome young man extracted himself from the bucket seat and stood, gazing at his audience through expensive sunglasses. He removed the glasses, bestowing a crooked, incredibly charming grin on all of them. "Good afternoon, ladies. I didn't expect such a gorgeous welcoming committee."

Grace was tempted to refute his assumption since it was pure happenstance that they were out here, but she managed to hold back her comment. She rose. "You must be Dylan Prescott. How nice to meet you." Time to put on her innkeeper hat and get Dylan checked in. Judging by the stupefied look on Charlotte's face, it was obviously up to her.

"How's it going?" Grace entered the kitchen with Winston at her heels.

Charlotte was rolling slices of roast beef for a meat platter. "Not too bad." She gestured at a big bowl of greens and an array of small side dishes already prepared on the counter. "Although I did make a spreadsheet, like I said earlier. They can all eat fruits and vegetables. Then I'll have meat, cheese, and hummus on the side for protein."

"Thankfully that doesn't sound terribly difficult," Grace said. "But if we eat the same menu as our guests this week, I think there will be some weight loss around here with a break from the delectable scones, pancakes, pies, and other treats you usually whip up. Not that I wanted such a break."

Charlotte laughed. "Don't despair. In a day or two, I'll figure out how to make tasty treats that are vegan and gluten-free." She pursed her lips. "Some condiments have gluten, so I'm making my own mayo and ketchup. And salad dressing, but of course I usually do that anyway."

"No creamy ranch, though," Grace said with a sigh. "Or green goddess." She adored Charlotte's homemade dressings. They were so much better than store-bought.

"Tell you what." Charlotte pulled a piece of plastic wrap off the roll. "Once they check out, I'll make you an eggy, creamy meal, including homemade bread and dessert."

"It's a deal," Grace said. She glanced at the clock. "Time for your dinner, Winston."

The little dog danced and panted as if to say, "No kidding."

She poured kibble into his bowl, wondering fleetingly if it was gluten-free. Now she had special diets on the brain.

Winston bounded over to his bowl and began eating.

Charlotte tucked the plastic wrap around the meat platter. "So where's our first guest?" A hint of pink in her cheeks betrayed her curiosity about Dylan.

"He's wandering around the inn checking out all the original features," Grace answered. "He appreciates staying in such a 'historic treasure,' as he put it."

"He seems okay," Charlotte said. "I wonder why their lawyer warned us."

So did Grace. Before she could respond, her phone beeped. She pulled it out and checked the screen. "Oh, good. That was Phillip

Watson. The rest of the guests are five minutes away. He says they're ready for dinner."

"Showtime," Charlotte sang out. "Help me get this food into the dining room, will you, please?"

3

Charlotte

Charlotte stood back and regarded the dinner buffet. Not bad for pulling something together in a hurry. They were fortunate that even at this time of year they could still get fresh produce grown by local farms. The tomatoes, broccoli, and greens were gorgeous.

Dylan Prescott wandered into the room, and upon spotting Charlotte, he approached the buffet table. "That looks good," he said, motioning toward the pile of roast beef. "May I?"

"Help yourself," Charlotte said. "If there's anything special you want to eat during your stay, please let me know." With what the family was paying, she could certainly give them custom meals.

He grabbed a roll of roast beef and bit into it, eyeing her with speculation. "I read your bio in the back of your cookbook. Impressive."

The inn sold signed copies of Charlotte's cookbooks, and there was a display in the foyer near the front desk.

"Thanks. I like writing them." Feeling her cheeks heat at the compliment, Charlotte pretended great interest in rearranging tiny bowls of nuts, seeds, and dried fruit.

"I'll bet," Dylan said as he continued to watch her.

Charlotte wished the other guests would come in. She could hear their voices in the foyer.

"You grew up around here," he continued. "So you must be pretty clued in on what's what."

Here it comes, Charlotte thought with a sigh. Running her hands down her apron, she turned to face him. He really was blindingly handsome. But while she appreciated good looks, she preferred substance. Something about Dylan's manner told her that he skated on the surface of life. "It depends what you're asking about," she said lightly.

He glanced around, then asked, "Do you know about the home we're building for a needy family?"

"No, I don't," Charlotte said, tipping her head toward the doorway. Grace was entering the room along with an older gentleman. "But my sister, Grace, does. She's on the committee leading the project."

Dylan glanced at Grace, then returned his attention to Charlotte. "I'll talk to her later." Sidling a little closer, he asked, "What do people do for fun around here?" Throwing a glance at the older man, he added, "Young people, I mean."

Charlotte smiled. She doubted he was asking about fishing or biking or even strolling through the picturesque downtown, all pursuits many guests enjoyed. "The Tidewater on the other side of the lake is really nice. Sometimes musicians play in the evening."

Her good friend Dean Bradley owned and ran the inn and restaurant, renowned for its excellent food and conviviality.

"Good to know." Dylan winked. "Maybe I can buy you a drink later."

Grace's approach saved Charlotte from having to answer. "Charlotte, this is Phillip Watson, the coordinator of the group."

Charlotte greeted the attorney, then chatted about his trip and Magnolia Harbor's amenities.

Meanwhile, Grace talked to Dylan a short distance away. From her sister's body language, she could tell Grace was fending off questions. She tried to distract him with drinks, including both sweet and unsweet iced tea, water, coffee, and soft drinks.

"I got your instructions," Charlotte told Phillip. "I'll do my best to make sure that everyone is happy with the meals."

Phillip studied the platters of food. "If this is an example, I'll say that everything will be just fine." He lifted one brow. "Do forgive me for the delay in letting you know. I wasn't aware that my clients were so particular."

"It's fine," Charlotte assured him. "I enjoy trying new dishes. And I hope to provide some delicious ones during your stay."

Two women and a man entered the dining room, all three tapping away on their phones.

Dylan, who was filling a plate with meat and salad, said, "Why don't you give it a rest and eat, guys?"

The couple, still on their phones, wandered to a corner without responding.

Phillip turned to Charlotte and Grace and introduced the couple as Abel and Amy Butler and the younger woman as Savannah Prescott.

Pushing back glossy hair, Savannah approached the table, teetering on stiletto boots. She set down her phone and studied the food, then headed for the cheese tray. "Are these artisanal cheeses?"

"They are," Charlotte said. "Some of them are made locally at Roy Bevins's farm."

Savannah started at the mention of the farm but continued to focus on her food. "Are those rice crackers?" She frowned. "I can't eat gluten. It's not by choice, believe me."

Charlotte was relieved she'd bought the crackers, although at the time it wasn't because they were gluten-free. "They are. I'll be getting in some bread and other options for you too."

Savannah glanced at her as she loaded crackers with cheese. "That's so nice. This whole place is better than I expected."

Dylan snickered. "What do you mean? You thought Grandma might have us sleeping on pallets and eating gruel, like something in a Dickens book?"

"Yes, I did," Savannah admitted. "And I still can't believe I have to actually work as a farmhand. It sounds worse than my job at the mall food court."

"How long did that last?" Dylan sprinkled nuts over his salad, then picked up the dressing ladle. "Two days?"

"Three. And what can I say? It wasn't my thing. Too much grease." Savannah took some salad and followed her brother to one of the tables.

Winnie, who'd been helping them check in, bustled into the room holding a metal lockbox. Spotting Amy and Abel lurking near the fireplace, she made a beeline over to them. "Hello again." She opened the lid on the box and held it out. "It's time for your phones to go bye-bye. You'll get them back tomorrow morning for an hour."

Dylan smirked, his fork stalled halfway to his mouth. Savannah swiveled around in her chair, still chewing. Grace and Phillip watched in silence, the attorney's expression placid but interested.

Amy clutched her phone to her chest and glared. "Are you serious? I can't give up my phone. I've got a product going live at work."

"Me too," Abel said, furrowing his brow. "I mean, I need my phone, not that I have a product launching. But I can't miss an important message."

Winnie glanced at the clock, amusement dancing in her eyes. "It's seven o'clock. What in the world can possibly happen between now and tomorrow morning? Aren't businesses already closed?"

The couple exchanged glances.

"Well," Abel said, "it's not that something will happen . . ."

"It's more that we need to stay connected," his wife finished for him. "In our business, you can't afford not to be seen as a team player. My boss expects me to answer messages like *that*." She snapped her fingers.

"In tech, everything moves at lightning speed," Abel put in. "There's no time to waste. We have to rush products to market, or our competitors will get there first."

Winnie's gaze was sympathetic. "I realize that. But you're here to mourn your grandmother. People will understand if you're not constantly available."

A tense silence stretched out as Amy continued to cradle her phone, sneaking peeks at the screen and tapping at it.

Abel caved first. "Come on, hon. It's what your grandmother wanted. We can at least do that much for her." He dropped his phone into the box Winnie held.

"I suppose." Amy scowled like a child being punished. She stretched out her hand, letting the phone hover over the box, then snatched it back. "But no, I can't do it." She pointed at her sister. "Why does she get to keep her phone?"

That was a good question, and Charlotte was eager to hear the answer.

Everyone turned to Phillip, keeper of the rules.

He adjusted his collar and cleared his throat. "I'm not entirely sure, as I wasn't privy to your grandmother's decision-making process, but I do think it's because she wanted Amy and Abel to focus on each other." He cleared his throat again. "These devices can be a distraction, can't they?"

Charlotte agreed with that assessment. She'd seen people out on dates spend more time interacting with their screens than with the person across the table.

"Yeah, I don't have anyone to focus on right now," Savannah said, taking a big bite of salad. Speaking around the mouthful, she added, "Not that I couldn't if I wanted to. I'm always getting asked out." In between bites, she snapped photographs of her meal, Dylan's meal, and the dining room.

"So what's it going to be?" Phillip asked Amy. "Give your grandmother's wishes a try?"

Abel put an arm around his wife. "We can do it. Together."

As Amy regarded Abel, her face shone with hope. "You think so?" She sighed deeply as she carefully set her phone in the box. "Until tomorrow."

Winnie snapped the lid closed and spun the combination buttons in a flash. "See you tomorrow morning." She tucked the box under her arm. "Have a good night, all. I'm heading home."

Grace accompanied her to the front door.

"Let's eat," Abel said to Amy, guiding her over to the buffet table. He turned to Charlotte. "Just to let you know, we're vegan."

"So I understand," Charlotte said. "For tonight, I've put out two types of hummus for protein. I'll be expanding the menu tomorrow after I do some shopping."

"Thanks." Amy gave the chef a hesitant smile. "I know it's a hassle making all these different menus."

"No problem," Charlotte said, then glanced at Phillip.

The attorney sent her a silent thank-you. He picked up a plate and got in line behind the couple.

While they filled their plates, Charlotte tidied the table, thinking about her own meal. She and Grace would eat after the guests were finished, and then she'd clean up and prep for the morning. She'd better peruse her recipes and find breakfast items that would suit everyone.

A loud buzz erupted from Charlotte's pocket. Her phone. She'd completely forgotten it was in there.

Everyone turned to stare, especially Amy, who had a slightly lost look about her after being deprived of her phone.

"Excuse me," Charlotte said. She stepped out into the foyer, where Grace was behind the counter. Charlotte gave her a wave, then checked the screen.

Her heart lifted. Dean had texted her. After a period of being chef rivals earlier in their careers, now they inspired each other to new culinary heights.

Want to go to the farmers market with me tomorrow? he wrote. *I have a favor to ask and thought it would go over better while we're there.*

Charlotte smiled. She loved going to the local farmers market, even though it was winding down at this time of year. She quickly texted back and agreed to meet him. It would be a good opportunity to buy more local food for their guests, although Hanson's Farm Fresh Foods, her preferred market, also carried a great selection. She needed to stop there too.

Grace strode across the lobby, holding several pieces of paper. "How's it going?"

"Fine. They're all eating," Charlotte said. "What do you have there?"

Her sister waved the papers. "Agendas for our guests."

"Wow, their time here is structured," Charlotte commented, following Grace toward the dining room.

"Yes, it is." Grace halted to whisper, "And it's going to be quite interesting."

When they entered the dining room, Grace handed out the papers to the three siblings.

"What's this?" Dylan asked in between bites of food. Judging by what was on his plate, he'd gone back for seconds.

"These are your agendas for tomorrow," Grace said. "Dylan, you'll be going over to the construction site. Amy and Abel, you have free time in the morning and a pottery lesson in the afternoon. And, Savannah, you need to get outfitted for your volunteer job, then go over to the farm."

"Outfitted?" Savannah's eyes lit up. She scanned the page and frowned. "What's this? Rubber boots and overalls? Are you serious?"

"Well, you can't wear heels to shovel cow manure," Dylan said. He gave his sister a complacent smile.

Savannah's mouth dropped open. "Seriously? I'm supposed to deal with cow manure? What kind of farm is this?"

Charlotte turned away to hide a smile, but Dylan laughed outright and even Amy cracked a grin. Savannah obviously didn't have much experience with farms. All farms required hard, dirty work. It was certainly rewarding but often physically taxing.

"Why don't you wait and see?" Grace suggested. "The farm has cows, yes, but they also grow vegetables and fruit and make cheese. I'm sure it will be fine."

Savannah made a face. "Why would Grammie do this to me?" she wailed. "I hate nature and animals and dirt. She couldn't have picked something worse for me if she tried."

Charlotte thought that was the point. She had a feeling that Dorothy Prescott had been a very wise woman when it came to the experiences that would benefit her grandchildren.

Even if they didn't understand that yet.

4

Amy

Amy scooped up the last bit of hummus on her plate with a carrot stick. "What do you want to do after dinner?" she asked her husband. As she had the entire meal, Amy had to force herself to chew and swallow. Everything was tasteless and dry, but she knew her state of mind was to blame, not the food. Abel was on his third helping.

She felt empty, almost weightless, as if she were missing a limb instead of a phone. But the device was her connection to the world, its contents and communications often more compelling than what was right in front of her.

A whisper of understanding about Grammie floated through her foggy brain. Then it was gone.

"Did you hear me?" Abel asked. "I said, let's take a stroll around the garden. It's a nice night."

Amy studied his face, so familiar to her that she barely looked at him anymore. He was attractive, with lean features and skin that kept a tan all year. When they'd gotten married five years ago, she'd felt like the luckiest woman in the world. Now she just felt . . . indifferent. That was dangerous, she knew. Most women would snap Abel up in a heartbeat.

His dark eyes gleamed with concern as he returned her gaze. "Are you all right?"

"I'm fine." Amy glanced around the dining room. Everyone had left, except for the innkeepers, who were cleaning up the leftovers and dirty dishes. She and Abel should probably get going so as not to interfere with their work. "Let me run to our room and get a jacket."

Abel pushed back his chair. "I'll go with you." He gathered their plates and utensils and carried them over to a bus pan, earning smiles and thank-yous from Charlotte and Grace.

Amy led the way upstairs to the Dogwood Suite, which was gorgeous with its dark wood furniture and ivory walls. The bathroom was huge too. Grammie definitely had good taste when it came to choosing an inn. Inside, she went to her full suitcase, which was sitting unzipped on a rack, and began to root around for a fleece jacket.

"Are you going to unpack?" Abel asked. He'd already put away his clothing in the closet and bureau. He flipped through the hangers, then pulled down his fleece jacket.

"I'll do it after our walk." Amy tensed. How she organized her clothes was an ongoing bone of contention with the couple. She was a drawer stuffer while he was a neat freak who even folded his socks.

Abel disappeared into the bathroom, and she heard the electric toothbrush humming.

That was another thing. He brushed his teeth at least three times per day, more often if he had a snack. A wee bit obsessive? Perhaps. But did she criticize? No, of course not. The last thing Amy wanted to do was fight. It was easier to let things go. *And safer* . . . She frowned. Where had that thought come from?

Amy found her fleece jacket at the bottom of the suitcase and slid it on. Then her gaze fell on an envelope she remembered throwing on a side table. It had been placed exactly in the center, and the wrinkles had been smoothed out. Abel had struck again.

She crossed the carpet and picked it up, wanting to reread the letter from her grandmother. Well, it was more of a note. There was just a Bible verse and an assurance that Grammie loved Amy and believed in her.

For everyone to whom much is given, from him much will be required.

What could Grammie be talking about? Yes, Amy agreed that she'd been given a lot. She'd attended a private high school and had gotten an excellent college education. She'd traveled to Europe, skied and sailed, and had received a new car on her sixteenth birthday. Her grandmother had made all that happen, since Amy had been eight when her parents died.

Now Grammie was implying that Amy's response to all these gifts wasn't enough? She had a good job, a nice husband, and donated to church and charities on a regular basis. How much better could she be?

Frustrated, Amy crumpled up the paper, the reason it had gotten the first set of wrinkles. It wasn't fair. Grammie was raising all these issues, but Amy couldn't say anything or ask questions. Her grandmother had gotten the last word.

She pictured Grammie sitting on a cloud, smiling and wagging an admonishing finger, one of her customary gestures.

"I miss you," Amy whispered, her heart literally aching.

Abel bustled out of the bathroom. "Ready?" He'd taken the time to comb his hair and add fresh gel. Even after wearing his polo shirt and jeans most of the day, he still appeared crisp and put together.

In contrast, Amy felt like a tired old frump. For the drive from Atlanta to the inn, she'd changed into loose jeans, a baggy T-shirt, and sneakers. She thought of her fashionable sister, and a laugh escaped her lips. The only influence Amy would be on social media was for how not to dress.

"What's so funny?" Abel asked. He put his jacket on and zipped it up to the neck.

"Nothing," Amy said as she folded the letter and tucked it into her suitcase. "Just thinking about Savannah."

Abel went to the door and opened it. "Yeah, she's going to get a rude awakening at that farm. I can't picture your sister in muck boots."

Amy couldn't either. It appeared she wasn't the only one suffering from Grammie's odd and vague directives. She had that comfort at least.

Even in October, the evening temperature was in the fifties, and Amy and Abel were perfectly comfortable in their jackets and jeans. They silently strolled through the gardens, which held some late-blooming roses, camellias, and daylilies. But Amy smelled hints of leaves and earth mingling with the light fragrances, a sign that the growing season was winding down.

"Want to go down to the lake?" Abel asked.

"Sure," Amy said. The dark, gleaming water drew her gaze like a magnet despite the garden's beauty. Tonight the air was still, but wavelets washed against the shore in an unceasing rhythm. Amy was doing her best to calm her normally racing brain, to allow the peace of the scene to seep into her tight muscles and strained nerves.

Abel headed for the dock, where they found two Adirondack chairs and sat down side by side, still not speaking.

After watching the waxing moon rise over the water for a few minutes, he said, "This is really nice. Maybe your grandmother knew what she was doing after all." He chuckled. "Forcing you to relax."

His comment raised Amy's hackles. Another tender area in their marriage was Abel's tendency to point out what he regarded as Amy's weaknesses. He was always telling her that she was too tense and wound up.

Abel was one to talk. He'd had an almost meteoric rise at his firm due to long hours and his incredible genius mind, which never shut off that Amy could tell. Sometimes he'd be struck by inspiration in his dreams and get up in the middle of the night to work.

Amy thought long and hard about her response. She didn't want to start off their stay with a fight, despite his needling provocation. "Yeah, that's me. You have to tie me down to make me sit quietly." Her voice sounded calm, even amused, she noticed with relief.

She recalled playing with her toys as a child, doing her best to ignore the strife of angry voices drifting over her head like black clouds. Her parents had larger-than-life personalities. Her mother charmed everyone she met, and her father was everybody's best friend. But they clashed often. They also kissed and hugged each other and their children all the time.

It was her parents' fighting she remembered most, and sometimes it was the tiniest things that set off an argument. And then one day after a huge blowout, they'd never come home. The small plane they were in had crashed on a mountaintop.

The grief was timeworn and familiar now, a small ache Amy always carried. But the loss of her grandmother was sharp and fresh, and at remembering it, she gasped aloud. It would be like that for a while until her mourning became another soft sorrow she carried.

Abel grabbed her hand. "Are you okay?" In the moonlight, his face was carved like marble. "I'm such a jerk sometimes."

"No, you're not," she whispered. He was loyal, reliable, and caring, and his flaws were actually quite minimal compared to those of other men.

A small hope stirred in her heart. Could they find each other again and reignite the outrageous love they had shared five years ago? Oh, she hoped so.

Otherwise, she might end up filled with regrets, mourning what might have been.

5

Savannah

Savannah's alarm went off way too early. She was not a morning person, and she never had been. Amy used to have to drag her out of bed to get ready for school.

She checked the time. Yep. Six o'clock. They were expecting her at nine to start her ridiculous stint as Farmer Jane, so she'd better get going. She had to stop at the farm supply store first to buy clothes and footwear.

With one foot sticking out of the blankets, Savannah paused, struck by the absurdity of shopping for clothing at a farm store. She was known for her edgy designer wardrobe and ultracool style. What would happen if word got out that she was wearing overalls? Her whole reputation and plan would be ruined.

Savannah wanted a job in New York, working for designers who would pay her to wear their clothes, attend fashion shows, and generally be the "face" of their brand. Plenty of other women were already doing it, and she couldn't think of a more enjoyable job. The saying about doing what you love so you'll never have to work a day in your life fit her to a tee.

After jumping in the shower and dressing in jeans and a top, Savannah went downstairs in search of coffee. The buffet table was set with plates, utensils, mugs, and bowls, but there was no food yet. She followed the sound of clanging to the kitchen.

Charlotte was pulling a frying pan out of a cupboard. She glanced up and smiled when she saw Savannah standing in the doorway. "Good morning. Coffee's on if you want some." She gestured toward the coffee maker, which was gurgling and spitting, almost done.

"Sorry to invade so early, but I've got to get going." Savannah stepped into the kitchen. "And I'd love some coffee." She waited until the last drops dribbled down, then poured a mug. "Would you like a cup?"

"I sure would." Charlotte removed a carton of eggs from the fridge. "Do you want something to eat? I can whip you up an egg or two. I'm afraid I don't have gluten-free bread for toast yet. I'm getting gluten-free flour and some baked products today."

"That's okay. I usually have yogurt and fruit. But scrambled eggs sound good." Savannah poured Charlotte a mug. "What do you want in your coffee?" She added a dash of cream to hers, then fixed the chef's the way she instructed and brought it to her.

"These eggs came from the farm," Charlotte said, cracking one into a white bowl. "You'll get to meet the chickens later."

Savannah laughed. There was an introduction she had never entertained. "Are you joking?"

Charlotte shook her head. "Roy and Gladys Bevins treat their chickens like pets, including giving them lots of attention and high-quality food. And the eggs are fantastic as a result." She held the bowl out to Savannah. "See how orange that yolk is? Factory-farmed eggs are pale yellow."

Savannah had to admire the sight of the vivid orange yolk against the pure white bowl. Her artist's eye wanted to snap a shot. Her pulse quickened as ideas and images began to churn. Maybe she could take a few photos for her social media account on the farm. Featuring perky chickens and sweet cows, maybe. People loved locally raised food. In fact, foodies were obsessed with finding the best and freshest.

Her belly rumbled agreeably. "I can't wait to taste those eggs."

Maybe working on the farm wouldn't be so awful after all.

Savannah revised that thought a short time later while browsing the aisles at the farm supply store. Somehow she'd ended up in the feed section, surrounded by bags of dusty grain rising to the ceiling. Vicious-looking farm implements lined the walls, and nearby aisles held poisonous pesticides and gruesome treatments for worms and other ailments.

She closed her eyes, visualizing her favorite boutique. The air scented with delicate essential oils, plush carpet under her feet instead of concrete, and racks of gorgeous clothes extending in every direction. *Ah, heaven.*

"Excuse me."

Savannah startled and opened her eyes. A tall young man with a sandy goatee stood behind a flat cart piled with bags of corn. Except for the scowl twisting his features, he was quite handsome. His outfit of jeans and a flannel shirt suited his muscular build. Farmer Dreamy, she dubbed him. Not that she'd ever date a farmer. There was no way.

She finally noticed that she was blocking his path. With an apology and the flash of a smile, she edged over to allow him room to get by.

Without another word, he moved to pass her.

"Can you tell me where the clothing department is?" Savannah asked. "I have to buy rubber boots. Do you believe it?" She held out one dainty foot as though to illustrate how wrong such an awkward item would be on her.

Lifting his brow, he glanced down at her foot, then back up to her face. "Yeah, it is hard to believe. You're actually going to work outside?" His tone held disdain.

Savannah laughed in response, although humiliation warmed

her cheeks. How dare he imply that she was too weak or lazy to work outside? She crossed her arms. "I'm stronger than I appear," she said with a sniff. "I lift weights. And I'm a hard worker too."

The man shook his head. "That's not what I—forget it, okay?" He started to push the cart forward again, then stopped. "That's right. You wanted to find the clothing department. It's on the other side of the store. Past the tack department."

She didn't respond.

He gave her a wry grin. "Saddles. You know, for horses."

Savannah lifted her chin and glared. "I know what tack is." *I do now, anyway.* "Thanks for your help." She strode off, shoes clacking on the concrete floor. What a jerk, even if he was the cutest guy in here.

Annoyance fueling her pace, she raced through the store and found what she needed. Two sets of overalls, three plain white T-shirts, and one pair of rubber boots later, she was on her way to the farm.

Savannah wasn't exactly sure what to do, so she went to the farmhouse. Someone there should be able to tell her. Carrying her purchases, she ascended three wide painted steps to the porch, dodging a sleeping basset hound sprawled out in her path.

He lifted his big head and gave a feeble bark, then flopped back down again.

Some guard dog, she thought, rapping on the door with the knocker, which was in the shape of a cow's head.

While Savannah waited for an answer, she took in the farm. A shingled farm stand stood by the driveway entrance, and around the house were fields, some fenced in. Behind the house were a large barn, smaller outbuildings, and a few greenhouses. Everything appeared neat and trim and freshly painted.

The front door opened, revealing an attractive older woman. She wore an apron over her pants and a top, and she carried the aroma of something sweet with her, like apple jelly. "Good morning," she said with a big smile. "You must be Savannah Prescott. I'm Gladys, Roy's wife. Welcome."

Warmed by the greeting, Savannah returned the smile. "Thanks for having me." She lifted her bag. "Is there somewhere I can change my clothes?"

Belatedly, the dog had realized she was a stranger and was now up on his stubby legs and barking.

Gladys gave a firm command. "Be quiet, Buster. She's a friend."

The dog gave one last bark before sniffing at Savannah's bare ankles.

"Oh, that tickles." She danced away from his inquiring nose and hurried into the house.

Gladys showed her to the half bath downstairs.

Savannah went inside and changed, folding her clothes and sliding them into the bag she'd brought, along with her shoes. Then she studied herself in the full-length mirror on the door.

Oh my. The white T-shirt fit okay, but the overalls sagged around her torso in a most unflattering manner, as if she'd suddenly gained twenty pounds. As for the ugly dark-green boots, she had to shuffle her feet to walk. Moving awkwardly and trying not to trip, she carried her handbag and real clothes out to the kitchen to find Gladys.

Roy's wife was standing at the stove, stirring a tall pot that gave off fragrant steam. She looked Savannah up and down, then nodded in approval. "All set?"

"I think so," Savannah said.

Gladys motioned to a coatrack by the back door. "You can hang your bags there. Go out that door and over to the big red barn. Roy and Logan will tell you what to do. Coffee break is at ten and lunch at noon."

After thanking Gladys, Savannah tromped outside and across the backyard toward the barn. Beyond a white rail fence, sleek brown cows grazed, and a couple dozen hens pecked and cackled inside a pen. She hadn't realized that chickens had so many different feathers—black and white, buff, red, plain black, pure white, and spotted gray.

How pretty, she thought, remembering what Charlotte said about the chickens being like pets. She wanted to touch their fluffy feathers.

Despite her resolve not to like the farm, Savannah pulled out her phone and snapped a few shots.

The chickens noticed her and charged toward the fence in full cry. They probably thought she had food.

"Sorry, chickies. Maybe I'll feed you later." Then she examined their beaks. But would they peck her feet and legs going after the food? That seemed like a real possibility. Abandoning the idea of patting one, she tucked away her phone and continued toward the barn's double doors, which were standing open.

Her boots didn't make any sound on the packed dirt, and as she drew closer, she heard male voices inside.

"Are you sure it's a good idea?" a man said in a smooth, pleasant voice. "You don't know anything about her. She might be a disaster."

Savannah froze. They had to be talking about her. A wash of relief ran over her like cool water. If the farmer didn't want her, then the lawyer couldn't make her stay here. She glanced toward the house, tempted to change back into her normal clothes and leave.

Another man chuckled, deep and rumbling with a warmth that drew Savannah despite herself. "It'll be okay. Dorothy was a good person. She actually had me overnight my products to her in the Georgia mountains. Do you believe it? She was so loyal and generous."

Her heart lifted at this praise for her grandmother. Grammie loved patronizing small businesses. Then she came down to earth with a thump. So they were talking about her, the other guy thinking she couldn't hack it. Well, she'd show him. Forgetting all about leaving, Savannah stomped toward the barn.

"Hello," she called when she stepped into a vast space with a loft above. To each side were rows of stalls, with troughs in front of them. The two men were standing to one side, and with a start of surprise, she recognized the younger man from the farm store. "What are you doing here?" she blurted.

"You two have met?" The older man stepped forward, a crutch under one arm. "Where are my manners? You must be Savannah Prescott. I'm Roy Bevins."

Savannah shook his calloused hand. "I am. Nice to meet you, Roy." If she emphasized *you*, who could blame her? She turned to the younger man, not holding out her hand. "And you are?"

"Logan Burke," he muttered. "I own a farm down the road. Just here helping Roy out since he's got a broken ankle."

Roy grimaced. "Yep, rookie mistake. Turned my ankle stepping into the milking parlor." He blew out air. "It's tough getting old."

Logan patted Roy's shoulder. "You're not old. You're an inspiration to the rest of us." To Savannah, he said, "Roy's got a model farm here. Not only award-winning food but self-sustaining too."

"Cut it out." Roy rubbed at his cheek, appearing embarrassed by the praise. "Savannah, we're glad to have you with us. I knew your grandmother, and she was a wonderful lady. I'm so sorry for your loss."

Savannah toed her boot into the barn floor, made of ancient boards and sprinkled with hay. It was interesting hearing what other people thought about Grammie. To Savannah, she'd been a loving but somewhat distant presence. Of course in recent years, Savannah hadn't spent much time with her at all. Unease stirred. Maybe some of that distance was her fault.

"Do you want to show Savannah the ropes?" Roy asked Logan. "I've got to hobble back to the house and put my foot up for a while." "Will do." Logan bared his teeth in a smile. "Ready to get started?" Savannah straightened. "I sure am. Lead on."

While Roy slowly crossed the barn, Logan took Savannah into the side area, the milking parlor. The cows were outside, but they'd left ample evidence of their presence behind.

Logan handed her a tool. "This is a barn scraper. You'll use this and a pitchfork to clean the area."

She felt her lip curling in disgust. "Seriously? Where do I put it all?"

He showed her a hatch. "Push it down here. That's where we store the manure."

"You keep it? Why?" Savannah asked. She couldn't imagine storing a huge pile of cow output.

Logan crossed his arms, a mocking smile flitting across his lips. "We use it for fertilizer. Black gold, we call it. Don't you know anything?"

Angry humiliation rippled down Savannah's spine. "I know plenty about a lot of things. It's not my fault if I'm not a farm expert. Why would I be?"

"Fair enough," Logan said. "So, after you're done with this side, do the same on the other. Then I'll show you where the straw is. You spread out fresh straw in the clean stalls."

Savannah surveyed the length of the milking parlor and doubled it in her mind. It was going to take hours. But she merely nodded.

"Holler if you need me. I'll be at the house." Logan strode away without even a backward glance.

After sending him a glare he didn't see, Savannah got to work, trying to ignore pungent odors and the squishing under her boots. Soon she got into a rhythm, allowing herself to daydream about her new job in New York. It didn't exist yet, but she was sure it would soon.

Thank goodness no one she knew could see her right now, up to her ankles in unmentionable stuff. But it was going okay.

Until she slipped in a puddle and fell down on her hind end. It didn't hurt too much, since she landed on a pile of straw. But muck splattered her everywhere—her legs, her arms, and yes, even her face.

Savannah burst into tears.

6

Grace

"Good morning," Grace said as she entered the kitchen, Winston trotting behind her. Charlotte was putting final touches on breakfast. "Sleep well?" Grace asked, pouring a cup of coffee.

"I did." Charlotte's attention was on the fruit platter she was arranging. "I slept with my windows open. It was so refreshing."

"Me too," Grace said, stirring in cream. In the summer, they used air-conditioning most of the time, and even here in South Carolina, it got cold enough in winter to require heat. Fall and spring were the seasons when outside temperatures were ideal for sleeping. Grace took a big swallow of coffee, then glanced down at the eager dog. "Hold on, Winston. Your breakfast is coming right up."

He wagged his tail so hard that his whole body wiggled, making both women laugh.

"I wish everyone was so easily satisfied," Charlotte said. "I'm definitely playing it by ear this morning."

"Got to love dogs." Grace opened the cupboard and grabbed the dog food. "They'll eat almost anything you put in front of them." She gave Winston high-quality food, of course. As a result, he was happy and healthy, with silky fur and clear eyes.

Charlotte added the last chunks of fresh pineapple to the platter, which also held blueberries, strawberries, and kiwi. "Want to carry this out for me? We're almost ready to serve." She dashed back to the stove to stir a pot of something and check on a pan of scrambled eggs. Bacon already sat draining on paper towels.

"Sure thing." Grace finished with Winston, then washed her hands. "I see you're making a couple of different breakfasts." Usually there was a fixed menu offering both cold and hot dishes. But to satisfy their guests' dietary needs, Charlotte was making two hot breakfasts.

"That's right," Charlotte said. "Oatmeal for the vegans and scrambled eggs and bacon for Dylan and Phillip. Savannah already ate and left."

Grace picked up the fruit platter. "Oh, I almost forgot she had to go over to the farm. I wonder how that's going."

Charlotte grinned. "I'll bet we'll hear a full report later. She's certainly outgoing enough to share her thoughts."

"Hey, ladies," Dylan said, his voice gravelly from sleep. "Is that coffee I smell?" He yawned and stretched, then ran a hand through his disheveled hair. Even this early in the day, he was incredibly handsome, and the smile he bestowed on Charlotte told Grace he knew it.

"Good morning," Grace said. "Follow me to the dining room, and I'll bring out the coffee carafe in a minute." She carried the platter into the other room and set it on the long table.

Dylan settled at the table. "This looks great." He began to select fruit from the platter with a fork. "I'm starving."

Grace wasn't surprised, since most young men had hearty appetites. "Charlotte's got bacon and eggs coming. And I'll get your coffee." Pitchers of juice and water were already on the table, which was set with dishes and silverware.

"What's the deal with the building project?" Dylan asked, popping a strawberry into his mouth.

"Spencer Lewis, who is in charge of the project, will be here before you go over to the site," Grace said. "He's going to fill you in."

Spencer, a good friend and retired intelligence analyst for the

FBI, lived nearby at Blossom Hill Farm. He had volunteered to chair the various committees that were helping to build and furnish the single-family home.

Dylan nodded, the lack of enthusiasm on his face telling. "I'm sure it's not going to be much of a challenge for me." He puffed out his chest. "The last project I designed was a high-rise in downtown Atlanta. Retail space, offices, and penthouse condos. Presales were through the roof."

"Sounds impressive," Grace said politely. The four-bedroom split-level brick ranch the Halstead family had chosen could probably fit in one of those penthouse apartments. Regardless, the hardworking construction team would not appreciate a condescending attitude. Grace hoped Dylan would be wise enough to temper that.

Dressed in khakis and a long-sleeved polo shirt, Phillip entered the room, a pleasant fragrance of aftershave wafting from him. "Lovely morning. How is everyone?" He ambled over to the table and sat down opposite Dylan.

Dylan only grunted an answer.

Grace smiled at the attorney. "I'm fine. Thank you for asking. Breakfast will be served shortly. Bacon and eggs or oatmeal. In the meantime, would you like a cup of coffee?"

"Bacon, eggs, and yes, coffee, please." Phillip flapped a cloth napkin open and set it on his lap.

"I'll be right back with the coffee." As Grace left the room, she heard Phillip ask Dylan if he was ready to begin the building project. She didn't linger to hear Dylan's answer.

"Two for bacon and eggs," Grace told Charlotte in the kitchen. "Phillip is in the dining room. And I think he'll take toast, even if Dylan doesn't. As will I." She couldn't imagine not having toast with her eggs.

"Got it," Charlotte said. She started putting the food on plates.

Grace delivered the coffee carafe to the dining room, then returned to the kitchen.

A knock sounded on the back door, causing Winston to bark.

"I can guess who that is," Grace said. Spencer usually came to the back door when he stopped in.

Grace and Winston went together to answer the door, Grace's heart lifting when she saw she was right. The widower, with his easy smile and attractive features, was a welcome sight any day.

"You're just in time for breakfast," Grace said.

Spencer ran a hand over his salt-and-pepper hair, that easy smile turning slightly sheepish. "To be honest, I was hoping you'd say that. I could never turn down an opportunity to eat Charlotte's cooking."

Grace smiled as she opened the door wider. "Come on in."

After Spencer stepped inside, he bent to give Winston his due, the small dog wiggling all over with joy. Then Spencer and Winston followed Grace to the kitchen, where Charlotte was putting together the platters of food to be served family style.

"White or wheat?" Charlotte asked Spencer after saying hello. At his response, she nodded for Grace to add a couple more slices to the toaster. "I'll bring in platters of food in a jiffy," the chef said. "Grace, why don't you go ahead and eat with Spencer?"

"I think I will," Grace said, then turned to Spencer. "We can catch up on the house project over breakfast."

"Any sign of the lovebirds?" Charlotte asked, referring to Amy and Abel.

Grace shook her head.

"Let me know when they come down, and I'll bring out their oatmeal."

"Will do," Grace said.

They wandered out to the dining room, where Spencer filled a mug of coffee and Grace added more to her cup before joining the two guests.

"Breakfast will be right in," Grace said. She introduced Spencer. "He can tell you about the project over our meal, Dylan. Then we'll head over to the site."

"Oh, are you involved, Grace?" Phillip asked. "It sounds like quite an undertaking."

"It is," Grace said. "We're mostly volunteers, and Spencer is tasked with keeping us all on schedule."

Spencer chuckled. "Like herding cats, as they say. But at least they're well-meaning cats. By using volunteer crews, we're able to do the project relatively inexpensively. Of course, professionals oversee the teams and are installing the plumbing, HVAC, and electrical."

"My team is doing the interior design," Grace said. "We're working with the family to pick out colors and materials for the floors and walls, as well as the appliances and furniture. It's really fun." She'd watched a lot of home improvement shows for inspiration. Renovating and decorating her historic inn was quite different from a modern family home.

"You have an architect, I hope," Dylan put in. "Even if it is a small project, it's critical to start with a good set of plans."

Although the young man's tone held a challenging edge, Spencer didn't seem to take offense. "We sure did. A very reputable architect drew up the plans for us pro bono." He named the firm, which made Dylan's eyes widen. "I'll get you a set of blueprints if you'd like to see them."

Dylan pursed his lips and shrugged as if indifferent to the offer.

His gesture got Grace's dander up.

Fortunately, Charlotte entered the room right then, carrying platters of food. Grace leaped up to help.

"We've got bacon and scrambled eggs, both locally sourced," Charlotte said to the guests. "And toast for those who eat grains." She went to the sideboard and grabbed a stand holding three small jars. "Honey, jam, and apple butter for toast." She placed the stand in the middle of the table.

As the platters were passed around, Amy and Abel appeared in the doorway, both of them still clearly sleepy.

Amy's gaze went right to Grace. "Can we get our phones now?"

Grace exchanged a glance with Charlotte. It was telling that Amy's first comment concerned her phone, not greeting anyone, including her brother, or asking about food or coffee.

"Winnie has them, and she should be here any minute."

Her aunt had taken the locked box home with her, as an extra precautionary step, she guessed. It was hard to imagine that the couple would be desperate enough to break into a locked box, but Grace supposed anything was possible.

"I made oatmeal for you, and we've got a fruit platter," Charlotte said. "Coffee is on the sideboard, and there is also hot water for tea. A selection is here." She showed them the basket of tea bags. "I'll be right back with your oatmeal, if that's okay."

Amy and Abel nodded, with thanks Grace was glad to hear, and made their way to the sideboard. The couple whispered to each other as Abel poured his wife a mug of coffee and one for himself, then added non-dairy creamer to both mugs.

Grace turned her attention to the food, waiting until her guests helped themselves before filling her own plate.

Winnie entered the room, carrying the metal box. She beamed at the Butlers. "Ready for your phones?" Without waiting for an answer, she set the box down on a table and unlocked it.

Amy hurried over to join Winnie, coffee mug still in hand. "Oh, thank you." She snatched up her phone. "I can't wait to check my messages." She sank into the closest chair, set her mug down, and began to tap away.

"And she's gone." Dylan snickered before shoveling another forkful of eggs into his mouth. He'd heaped his plate and was systematically working his way through the pile. After swallowing, he asked Spencer, "So why are we building a house for these people? Who are they?"

"The Halstead family." Spencer's expression grew somber. "Their old house burned down."

Dylan stared at Spencer. "Huh," he finally said. "What happened? Someone smoking in bed?"

An uneasy silence fell over the table. Grace almost choked on her toast, and even placid Winnie, pouring herself a cup of coffee, appeared taken aback.

Phillip threw his napkin down. "That's quite an assumption, Dylan. I'm not im—"

Spencer put up a hand and nodded to let Phillip know he'd take the ball. "The wiring was defective due to the landlord's negligence," he said, his voice calm but forceful. "The smoke detectors also weren't working. If it wasn't for the intervention of the family dog, who woke them up, they all would have died. An older woman, a single mom, and two young teens."

Grace had heard the story before, but still her heart shivered at the realization that an enormous tragedy had been so narrowly averted. She sent a prayer of gratitude heavenward.

The others in the room appeared profoundly impacted, even Amy, who glanced up from her phone, frowning. "That's awful."

Dylan shifted in his seat. No trace of snide bravado now. "That is rough. Glad it worked out okay for everyone."

"It did, by the grace of God," Spencer said. "And that's why we're all so blessed to help the Halsteads by building them a new home. One with hardwired smoke detectors with battery backups."

"As they should be," Dylan remarked with a snort.

There was silence for a few moments until Spencer asked Phillip a question about college football. That nicely diverted the conversation for a while.

Then Spencer filled Dylan and Phillip in on the construction schedule. They hoped to take a huge leap forward this week. Dylan questioned the schedule. But Spencer mentioned another charity program with a world record of three hours to build a house. Their goal was much more modest by comparison.

After breakfast, Grace helped Charlotte clean up the dining room.

While Charlotte went to the farmers market to meet Dean, Grace rode with Spencer and Dylan to the construction site. Enough people came and went from the site that she'd easily be able to catch a ride back to the inn. Besides, she wanted to keep an eye on Dylan and see how he handled his assignment.

The Halstead home was located just outside of downtown Magnolia Harbor in a neighborhood of modest but well-kept and attractive homes with large yards. A neighborhood featuring basketball hoops, dogs, and children riding their bicycles. The location wasn't far from the junior high and high schools, which would be handy for the teens.

Workers were already at the site, where the foundation was ready for framing. A pile of lumber sat near the building, tarps protecting it from the weather.

Spencer waved at the crew and pulled into a spot in between two pickups.

When they all got out of Spencer's car, Grace spotted Julep

Buckley's vintage Cadillac parked along the street, which meant her committee members were already here.

"I'll introduce you to the team," Spencer told Dylan.

The two men walked over to where workers in hard hats were conferring.

Grace saw Julep, a local historian, and Helen Daley, the police captain's wife, standing off to one side watching. Next to them was a folding table holding carafes of hot drinks and platters of pastries. Bottled water on ice filled a cooler next to the table.

"How are you ladies this morning?" Grace asked as she approached them.

After everyone exchanged greetings, Julep remarked in her typical dry way, "I see Spencer has a new sidekick."

"Who is that good-looking young man?" Helen asked, tucking a strand of blonde hair behind her ear. "I don't recognize him as local. And there was a time when I knew all the young people in town." She had two grown sons who now lived in other states with their families.

Grace explained who Dylan was, tactfully saying that he was doing community service at the behest of his grandmother.

"Ah yes, Dorothy Prescott." Julep's pleasantly lined face was sad. "She was quite a gal. Always ready to help out, checkbook open. She would have loved to support this project."

"Tell me more," Helen said. "I don't think I ever met Dorothy. Wasn't she a sponsor of the pottery festival?"

The three women chatted while helping workers who wandered over for refreshments.

Spencer and Dylan donned hard hats, and soon orders were being shouted as the first pieces of lumber were put into place. The structure's frame quickly took shape, which Grace found fascinating. They'd gone from nothing to something within a couple of hours.

Other volunteers for the food booth arrived, and Helen got ready to head home. Grace was about to ask her for a lift to the inn when a van pulled up.

Julep took Grace's arm. "The Halsteads are here. Have you met them?"

"Only in passing," Grace said. She'd seen the family at the kickoff dinner for the project at Fellowship Christian Church. "We should schedule a meeting with them to discuss interior design after we hash out some ideas. We can meet at the inn with Charlotte doing refreshments, if you think that's okay."

"That sounds lovely, dear. Come with me." Julep led the way over to the van.

Kelli Halstead, a woman a little older than Charlotte, hopped out of the vehicle. She had light-brown hair and a friendly smile. She opened the side door, and Etta, her mother, climbed out. Mia, Kelli's teenage daughter, followed with her long dark hair swinging. Then a wheelchair rolled down a ramp from the open door. Evan, Kelli's bright and funny thirteen-year-old son, was seated in it.

The workers munching on doughnuts and drinking coffee nearby glanced over at the family, Spencer and Dylan among them. Grace thought she saw a flash of sympathy cross Dylan's face at the sight of Evan, which was a plus in his column.

Next, a small gray sedan came down the street and parked right behind the van. A moment later, a young woman emerged, slinging a purse over her slender shoulder. Attractive, with a blonde ponytail and freckles across a pert nose, she was dressed casually in jeans, a windbreaker, and sneakers.

"Who is that young woman?" Grace asked. "I don't recognize her."

Julep followed her gaze. "Tabitha Douglas, a social worker. She's been helping the Halsteads get the services they need."

From the way Tabitha greeted the family, getting a hug from Mia and a fist bump from Evan, Grace guessed she was more than just a government official to them.

She and Julep had reached the little group, and Julep said, "I'd like you all to meet my good friend Grace Porter."

While Grace was being introduced, Spencer and Dylan joined them. More introductions followed.

"You're an architect?" Evan asked Dylan.

When Dylan nodded, Evan proceeded to ask him all kinds of questions about how he'd become an architect and what his job was like.

At first Dylan seemed uncomfortable by Evan's outspokenness, but he eventually warmed to the boy. Grace had the feeling that Dylan hadn't been around many kids.

Then Dylan met the attractive Tabitha, and he appeared awestruck.

For her part, the social worker kept it strictly business while shaking Dylan's hand. "This project is a real blessing," Tabitha said in her soft voice. "Not only are we helping out a wonderful family, but we're coming together as a community." Her blue eyes had an inquiring expression, as if she really cared about his thoughts. "It doesn't get any better than this. Don't you agree?"

"Absolutely," Dylan mumbled, his face reddening.

His arrogant attitude was nowhere to be found.

7

Amy

Amy tapped away on her phone. "Just a minute," she told Winnie, who was standing nearby with that infernal box. The hour was up, Amy's breakfast was cold, and she still had a dozen e-mails to respond to.

"Give it a rest." Abel spread jam on a piece of toast. Charlotte had assured them that the bread contained no eggs or milk. "You'll get the phone back tomorrow."

"I can't believe how calm you are." Amy glared at her husband. "Last night you were complaining about this rule Grammie imposed on us."

Abel chewed and swallowed before answering. He never talked with his mouth full. "It made me more efficient. I got all the important stuff done." He'd already turned his phone off and returned it to the box.

"All right, that will have to do." Amy switched off her phone with a huff, then placed it in the box. "Satisfied?"

Winnie closed the lid and locked the box. "I'm not the one you need to satisfy," she said, her gentle smile taking the sting out of her words. She reached into her pocket and pulled out an odd object. Made of wood, it was about eight inches long and capped on both ends with wire loops. "This is for you."

"What is it?" Amy asked. She turned the object around in her fingers, studying it. Without her phone, she couldn't even do an image search and find out.

"I have no idea, but I think you'll need it." With that cryptic remark, Winnie picked up the box, wished them a good day, and left the dining room.

Abel took the tool and waved it at Amy. "She's an interesting woman. I'll give her that." He set the item down and picked up his mug. "Are you ready to roll?"

Amy stared at the cold, congealed oatmeal in her bowl. "Yeah, I guess so. What do you want to do this morning?"

They were scheduled to go to the arts center in the afternoon. But until then they had hours of free time that seemed to stretch endlessly, like an empty landscape. When was the last time she had found herself with nothing to do, no obligations? Their honeymoon five years ago? She couldn't remember.

"I thought we could go kayaking," Abel said. "I saw some kayaks down at the inn dock."

Amy gazed out the window toward the lake. It was a beautiful, sunny day, and the water looked fairly calm. She hadn't gone kayaking since she'd been at camp as a teen, and she remembered how much she had loved it. Why had she waited so long to do it again? She pushed back from the table. "Let's do it."

They were already wearing shorts and water sandals, so they were set to go on the lake. At Abel's suggestion, they stopped by the kitchen to get bottles of water and snacks, which Charlotte readily supplied. She also told them that the life jackets and paddles were stored in a small shed.

Abel carried the provisions, leaving Amy unencumbered. They walked outside and stepped across the grass toward the water. The air was still today, only a slight breeze tickling her hair. Even better, the temperature was already above seventy, and it was slated to reach eighty this afternoon. So it was warm enough to paddle without wearing layers of clothing.

After donning life jackets and selecting paddles, they carried the long but fairly light craft to the dock, one on each end, and lowered it into the water.

"Go ahead and get in." Abel directed her to the front seat. "I'll push off."

Amy climbed in a little awkwardly, remembering to distribute her weight evenly and quickly to avoid tipping over. "All set." She gripped the dock with both hands to keep the boat stable.

He deftly climbed aboard, sliding into the seat without rocking the kayak too much. "This is fun already."

Abel used his paddle to push them away from the dock, and Amy copied his movements. Then they paddled out toward deeper water.

At first everything went fine. Amy allowed Abel to lead, and he told her which side to paddle on, which helped them glide smoothly through the water and turn when needed. Amy sat back against the seat, savoring the combination of sunshine, fresh air, and gentle exercise. The shore and its problems receded until there was nothing but the beauty of water and sky all around her.

They were quite far out in the lake when the breeze began to strengthen.

"The wind's picking up," Abel said. "We should probably head back."

A thrill of alarm ran down Amy's spine. The inn appeared far away, only a tiny rectangle on the shore. They had to cross a huge expanse of water to reach it. She hadn't realized they'd gone so far. "Are we going to make it?"

Abel snorted. "Of course. We're not stuck in a storm or anything."

But as they traveled across the water, the wind grew stronger. It was coming right toward them, creating a headwind that hindered their progress.

To Amy, it seemed they worked and worked and didn't get

anywhere. Her shoulders began to burn, and her arms were limp with exhaustion. "I can't do it!" she cried, resting the paddle across the bow.

A large wave lifted and dropped underneath them, making the kayak roll back and forth.

"You have to!" Abel shouted. "And don't let a wave hit the kayak broadside, or we'll go over."

"Yes, sir," Amy muttered, stung by his tone. She picked up the paddle and dug in, her muscles marginally recovered. They couldn't even call for help, since their phones were locked away. In addition, the lake was practically deserted, with only one or two fishing boats out. They were at a distance, so no help was forthcoming there.

On and on they paddled, only fierce determination spurring Amy on despite the flaming agony in her upper body. What choice did they have? They couldn't stay in the middle of the lake. Foot by foot, they made slow progress.

At long last the dock was within view, the sight as heartening as the first sight of a desert oasis. A promise of sanctuary and safety, of comfort and ease. Amy never wanted to kayak again. No, it was dry land for her all the way.

"Paddle on the left," Abel called.

Amy didn't agree with that order, so she ignored him and paddled on the right. But they veered sharply off course.

Then Abel started paddling on the right as well, and their paddles hit with a bone-jarring clash.

They both started yelling suggestions, and having lost their rhythm, they were unable to get back in sync. Bigger waves, small breakers really, were now rolling in. For a long, helpless moment, the kayak rocked from side to side, the motion making Amy seasick.

Abel's yells grew even more frantic as he fought to control the craft.

Then, in less time than it took for her to realize what was happening, the kayak flipped over, spilling them into the lake.

Cold water enveloped Amy as she sank below the surface, bubbles streaming from her mouth. Before she had time to panic, the blessed, buoyant life vest pulled her out of the water and into the fresh air and sunshine.

She glanced around for Abel and saw him holding on to one end of the overturned kayak.

"Are you okay?" he asked, his tone sharp with fear.

"I'm fine. Good thing I had time to take a breath before I went under." With a laugh, she paddled toward the other end of the boat and began tugging it toward shore.

Being wet wasn't pleasant, but she was alive.

Soon they were able to stand on the rocky, mucky bottom, and from there it was a simple matter to beach the kayak. They left it turned over on the grass to drain and dry, the wet life jackets beside it, and stowed the paddles in the shed.

"We'd better get changed," Amy said, her feet squishing with every step. The breeze was cooling her wet clothing off fast, making her teeth chatter.

Abel slung an arm around her shoulders and dropped a kiss on top of her head. "I was really scared out there." His voice was husky. "I'm sorry I yelled."

At his apology, a lump of hurt and anger began to dissolve in her heart. "Me too. Scared and sorry both. But we had our life jackets, and they did the job." She laughed. "Not that I wanted to put them to the test."

Abel chuckled. "Neither did I."

With his arm still around her, they squelched across the grass.

"I'm not sure what we're doing here," Abel said. "But I do know one thing. We haven't been spending enough time together. And I miss that. I miss us."

"So do I," Amy whispered.

The warmth emanating from Abel, even though he was wet, was comforting and welcome as they sloshed along. The two of them, both type A personalities, had forgotten how to have fun together, to relax and enjoy each other's company. She plainly saw that they had been living on parallel tracks, charging ahead toward individual destinations.

Would they be able to align their ambitions before it was too late?

8

Savannah

Savannah used the back of her hand to wipe her eyes.

She sat there in the middle of the barn, wearing a hideous outfit that was soaked and dirty. Thank goodness her social media followers couldn't see her now. She'd be laughed right off the Internet. As for the job she was hoping to get, it would be gone as quickly as she'd slipped and fallen.

For some reason, the Bible verse her grandmother had given her flashed into Savannah's mind. *Turn away my eyes from looking at worthless things, And revive me in Your way.*

"Is everything okay in here?" Logan called. "Where are you? It's time for a coffee break."

Savannah cringed. She certainly didn't want Logan to see her like this. Wrinkling her nose in disgust and thankful for gloves, she pushed herself off the milking parlor floor. Her entire seat and the back of her overall legs were wet. What was she going to do? She couldn't work this way.

"Oh boy. What happened to you?" Logan clapped a hand over his mouth, but that didn't stop Savannah from noticing the twinkle in his eyes. He was obviously trying to hold back laughter.

Attempting not to let the wet denim touch her skin while taking tiny steps in her rubber boots, Savannah walked toward him. "What do you think? Are you going to help me or laugh at me?"

He took her in for a long moment, his hand now stroking his chin. The way his lips were moving, she guessed he was expending quite an effort not to give in and guffaw. He swallowed, his Adam's apple bobbing, and said in a hoarse voice, "Come to the house, and we'll find you a change of clothes."

Savannah glanced down at her overalls. "You think Gladys wants me anywhere near her spotless house? I don't think so. I can change in here somewhere." She tugged at her pant leg. "And these can be burned or something."

Logan pointed at her. "Good point. Hold on. I'll be right back." Once he was out of sight, Savannah heard a huge bellow of laughter.

But instead of being mad, she found herself laughing too. What else was she going to do? Sometimes the only way through an awkward situation was to laugh.

While Savannah waited for him to return, she started cleaning the stalls again, finally getting into a rhythm that maximized her effort. The neat side of her nature took pleasure in each foot of progress.

"Wow, you're doing great," Logan said. He stood behind her with an armful of folded clothing. "Gladys sent these out. She said she'd put yours in the washer. Get changed, and we'll go take a break."

Savannah propped the scraper against a stall divider. "I can't believe it. She's so nice." Careful not to soil the new clothing by carrying it at arm's length, she found a room in the back that held harnesses and other equipment. It had a door that would give her privacy.

After changing and scrubbing up at the handwashing station near the milking parlor, she found Logan waiting by the big barn doors.

At the house, Gladys met them by the back door, holding out a hand for the overalls.

"I'm so sorry about this," Savannah said. "Thanks for washing them for me."

"Not a problem." Gladys winked. "You think this is the first pair of dirty overalls I've washed? Roy is a real slob."

"Hey, I resent that remark," Roy called from the kitchen.

"Go ahead and help yourself to coffee," Gladys said. "I'll put these in the washer." She disappeared through a doorway.

In the kitchen, Savannah found Roy seated at the round table, a mug of steaming coffee in front of him, the crutches leaning against the wall. She poured a cup of coffee and took a seat next to him.

Logan did the same and sat beside Savannah. He motioned to a plate of homemade oatmeal, chocolate chip, and molasses cookies in the middle of the table. "Want one?"

"No thanks," Savannah said. She was starving, but with her restrictions, she couldn't have one. She'd have to settle for the gluten-free bar she'd packed in her purse.

"You aren't watching your weight, are you?" Roy asked. "My wife's cookies have zero calories." He patted his belly and chuckled.

Gladys entered the room and went to the coffeepot. "Leave her alone. What she eats is her business."

"It's not that they aren't tempting," Savannah said. "But I can't eat gluten."

Gladys tipped her head. "Yeah, there's gluten in those. I used regular flour."

Logan reared back, studying Savannah with disbelieving eyes. "Is that really a thing? Next you'll be telling us you don't eat meat or eggs."

"No, that would be my sister," Savannah said. "She's vegan. Her husband too."

Roy shook his head. "If everyone went vegan, we'd be out of business."

Gladys sat at the table. "We do sell vegetables and fruit, so I suppose we could manage." She poured a little cream into her cup and stirred.

"It would be tough," Roy said. "Meat and eggs are our bread

and butter, so to speak." He reached for a molasses cookie and took a bite.

"These diets city people come up with nowadays," Logan said, grabbing a chocolate chip cookie.

Obviously he didn't worry about his weight. Not that he had to, as trim and strong as he was. Too bad he was so . . . something. She couldn't quite put her finger on it.

"I think it's all in their heads," Logan continued. "Too much time on the Internet."

An annoying know-it-all—that was the description she was searching for. And she couldn't let his remark slide by. "I'm sorry you don't approve," she said, using the sweet but steely voice she'd learned from Grammie. "But I have an actual digestive condition. If I ate gluten right now, well, it wouldn't be pretty." She smiled widely and batted her lashes. Score one for the city girl.

Roy grunted. "She got you there."

Logan gave a tiny nod of acknowledgment. "That sounds difficult to deal with." He swallowed the last of his coffee. "Let me know when you're ready, and we'll get back to work." He cocked one brow. "We're way behind."

Savannah decided to accept his challenge. She finished her coffee and set the mug on the tabletop with a thump. "Ready when you are." She gritted her teeth in determination. She'd show Logan that she was someone to be reckoned with, city girl or not.

Three hours later, Savannah headed back to the inn, every muscle aching. Her fresh and clean overalls, ready for the next morning, sat on the seat beside her. Her rinsed-off boots were in the trunk. But at least she wasn't hungry. Gladys had fed her a huge bowl of homemade vegetable soup for lunch.

She had to do it all over again tomorrow. And the day after that. Savannah had a vision of endless days stretching into the future, each one exactly the same. Milk, feed, out to pasture, clean, in from pasture, feed, milk, and settle for the night. Repeat.

How did Roy and Gladys stand the endless, mind-numbing routine? Roy had told her that he grew up on the farm and began helping when he was six, so that was probably the only life he knew.

As for Logan, Savannah gathered that he'd started farming by choice after obtaining an agriculture degree. He'd grown up in Charlotte, North Carolina, so his disparaging comments about city people were the pot calling the kettle black, as far as she was concerned.

Savannah was exhausted. Good thing it wasn't far to the inn, or she might fall asleep at the wheel. Her plan was to take a long, hot shower and relax for the rest of the afternoon. She definitely needed a break.

Soon she arrived at the inn entrance. Her spirits lifted as she pulled into the drive. What a beautiful place.

Winnie was behind the desk when Savannah entered. "There you are," she said. "How did it go at the farm?"

The experiences of the morning flew through Savannah's mind, both good and bad. "It was okay. But I'm really tired." She started to move toward the staircase. "I'm heading up to get some rest."

"Hold on a sec," Winnie said. "We're having a design meeting in half an hour on the veranda, if you'd like to join us."

Savannah paused, one foot on a step. "Design meeting?" The words called to her like a siren singing on a rock. "What kind of design?"

Winnie filed papers in a folder. "Interior design for the house your brother is working on." She closed the folder and slid it into a standing rack. "Seems like it might be right up your alley."

"Oh, it is," Savannah said fervently. "I'll be down in a few minutes." She ran up the stairs to her suite, her exhaustion dropping away.

After a quick shower, Savannah changed into one of her cutest outfits as an antidote to the memory of the overalls.

Struck by the beauty of the Buttercup Suite, she took a few pictures of herself next to the fireplace. She posted her favorite to her social media with the caption, *South Carolina dreaming in my suite at the Magnolia Harbor Inn.* She'd let her fans think she was on vacation, soaking up the ambience of this luxurious antebellum mansion.

To her satisfaction, likes began to flood in immediately. Maybe a few days playing farmer wouldn't derail her plans after all.

In a much better mood, she flew down the staircase, singing to herself. She followed the sound of voices out to the veranda.

Grace, Charlotte, Winnie, and an older woman were seated around a table, with swatches, paint chips, and design boards in front of them.

"Sweet and unsweet tea on the sideboard," Charlotte said. "And there are lemon cookies." She put a hand to her mouth. "Sorry. Forgot."

"It's all right," Savannah said, pouring a glass of sweet tea. "I have some gluten-free treats with me." She patted the little leather bag that was slung over her shoulder.

"I bought gluten-free flour today," Charlotte said. "I'll make muffins and cookies for you tomorrow."

"Sounds great," Savannah said as she settled into a chair. "Thank you."

Grace introduced Savannah to Julep Buckley.

"I'm so pleased to meet you," Julep said. "I knew your grandmother for many years. She was a wonderful lady."

Savannah mumbled thanks, recalling that Roy had said the same thing. How had she not known that Grammie had such a connection to this town?

The answer jumped into her head. Savannah had been so preoccupied with her own life that she'd barely paid attention to Grammie. Regret gnawed at her. Now Grammie was gone, and Savannah had missed the opportunity to learn from her, meet her friends, and hear about her passions.

"Kelli said with two energetic teens, she wants the house to feel restful but not boring." Grace held up a design board. "So this is what I came up with for the main living space. Gray as the main neutral with pops of turmeric orange and dusty red."

The women oohed and aahed as they admired the board.

"I love it. So classic but fresh and lively too." Julep made a face. "I feel like redecorating now. I still have wallpaper from the '90s."

"Grace is the best," Charlotte said, gesturing around the inn. "As you can see."

Savannah regarded the design board, agreeing that Grace had done a great job. But she felt that it could use a finishing touch. She remembered seeing something recently . . . She picked up her phone and searched for an image. "I love it too, but I think a touch of sunny gold would really round out the palette." She showed Grace the photo.

Grace studied the picture, then picked up a similar paint swatch and added it to the board. "You're right. It's perfect."

"What an eye you have," Winnie said to Savannah. "I know when a final product looks good, but I'm not quite sure how to get there."

Savannah sipped her tea, pleased at the compliments. This was what she was meant to do, not clean cow stalls.

What had Grammie been thinking?

9

Amy

In downtown Magnolia Harbor, Amy and Abel parked outside a brick building notable for huge windows and a sculpture garden to one side.

Abel's mouth dropped open. "Did you know anything about this?"

Amy was equally astonished. "No." She reached for the door handle. "I had no idea." She waited for Abel to get out and lock the car, then walked beside him to the entrance of the Dorothy A. Prescott Arts Center, as proclaimed in lettering installed on the brick facade.

How could this have happened without Amy knowing? A faint memory tickled at the back of her mind, her grandmother calling and leaving a message, saying she had exciting news about an arts center. But Amy had been on deadline, so she'd waited to call her back.

And then she had totally forgotten about Grammie's message until now when the evidence that she had been a lousy granddaughter was staring her right in the face—in very large letters too. Amy averted her eyes from the sign, hoping no one here made the connection and realized that she'd never bothered to visit before.

The lobby was spacious and two stories high, with balconies ringing the second floor. Paintings, pottery, and sculpture stood here and there. They were all nicely displayed.

A young woman with long dark hair greeted them from behind a tall counter. She wore a burgundy smock. "Welcome to the arts center. I'm Brianna Lawrence. How can I help you?"

Amy smiled at her. "We're Amy and Abel Butler, and we're here for a pottery class."

Brianna scanned the open appointment book on the counter. "Oh yes, here you are. You'll be working with me in the pottery room." She opened a half door and came out from behind the counter. "Follow me."

The trio walked down a corridor lined with classrooms and artwork on the walls. The place was almost dead quiet, the squeak of their shoes on the shiny tiles the only sound.

Amy glanced at each piece of art, all of them surprisingly good. Several colorful landscapes she liked were by an artist named Angel Diaz.

Brianna noticed her interest and smiled. "Isn't Angel's work amazing?"

"It certainly is," Amy said.

Even Abel, who had no artistic sense, agreed.

At the end of the hall was a huge pottery room with sections devoted to various parts of the process. To one side was a row of pottery wheels. Racks held drying items, tools, blocks of clay, and containers of glaze and paint. Long tables provided a place to paint or do handwork. In the back of the room were several kilns, the flickering red lights indicating that pottery was being fired.

"Have you ever worked with clay before?" Brianna asked as she handed them smocks from a cubby area.

Amy shook her head. "Not unless you count Play-Doh when I was a child."

"I haven't worked with clay at all," Abel said. "Art is not my thing."

Brianna seemed taken aback by his blunt comment, but she recovered quickly. "So you're a challenging student. Keep an open mind. You might discover that you like it." She led them over to one of the worktables.

"We're only here because we have to be," Abel remarked. "A family member set this up for us."

Amy frowned at him behind the instructor's back. If he didn't stop talking, he was going to embarrass her. What would Brianna think once she learned that Amy was Dorothy's granddaughter?

She stepped forward, hoping her expression appeared agreeable and interested. "Abel is correct, but I'm eager to learn. Isn't it good for your brain to try new activities, especially ones that use different skills?" She had no idea if that was true, but it sounded good. And she thought she'd read something along those lines.

Brianna laughed as she hefted a block of clay to the work surface, which was covered by a finely woven cloth. "I have no idea. But I do know that many of our adult students enjoy tapping into their creative side. For many of us, a few childhood art classes are our only exposure. Not only is it relaxing to make pottery, but it's also fun."

Abel didn't say anything else as he moved closer to the table to watch while Brianna cut chunks of clay from the block.

"We're going to start with simple handwork," Brianna said. "In a later lesson, you'll learn to use the wheel. But I want you to get a feel for the medium first." She held up her hands and grinned. "A real hands-on lesson."

The instructor rolled a chunk of clay flat with a rolling pin and trimmed the edges to make a rectangle. "We're going to make a dish using the pinch technique." Brianna demonstrated how she added shape to the clay pancake with only her fingers, making a shallow bowl. She placed a range of tools on the table. "These can be used to decorate your dish." With lightning fingers, she drew a lovely fern design inside the dish.

Amy glanced at her lump of clay, then the finished product. She thought it seemed simple enough. "I'm ready to try." She picked up the rolling pin.

"I'll leave you to it. If you need me, you can dial the front desk." Brianna showed them the phone and the directory. "Otherwise, I'll be in later to check on you."

After the door closed behind the instructor, Abel muttered, "That wasn't much of a lesson."

Amy was busy rolling out the clay—or trying to. It was stiff and hard to work with, not like biscuits or cookie dough. "I don't need any more instructions. It's easy. Besides, she had to start us at the beginning."

Abel laughed. "Yeah, like little kids." He snatched up his rolling pin and began attacking the hunk of clay.

Amy reached out to touch Brianna's dish to gauge the thickness. When her slab was thin and even enough, she trimmed the edges and began to pinch. But her dish came out lopsided and crooked. So much for her heritage as a pottery maker kicking in. Those genes must have died out or skipped over her. She'd always thought of herself as a creative person, but she normally dealt in the realm of ideas and concepts.

But how could she let a lump of clay defeat her? With new determination, she snatched up the rolling pin and rolled the mess flat. Then she began pinching again. This time, she did it more slowly.

"I'm taking a break," Abel announced.

Amy glanced up and saw a perfect dish sitting in front of him. "That's amazing."

Cracking a grin, he reached to scratch the back of his head. He stopped as he seemed to remember he had clay on his fingers. "I'm going outside for some air."

"I hope I'll be done soon." She went back to work.

He returned his smock to a cubby and walked out.

A little later, Brianna padded quietly into the room and joined Amy at the table. "How's it going?"

Amy cocked her head, considering. "Not too bad. But this is my third try." She was quite pleased with the effort, which might have been made by a junior high student instead of a preschooler. "What's next?"

Brianna carefully lifted the dishes Amy and Abel had made and put them on a shelf. "They have to dry before we can fire them in the kiln." She pointed to a row of bottles. "Then you pick out the glaze you want."

Amy cleaned up the table, then washed her hands and put away her smock. She walked out with Brianna. "When's the next lesson?" she asked when they reached the desk.

"Let me check." Brianna flipped through the appointment book. "You and your husband are scheduled for a wheel lesson tomorrow." She gave the particulars.

"Speaking of my husband, did you see where he went?" Amy asked.

Brianna pointed to the front door. "He's out in the sculpture garden making an important call, he said. I let him borrow my phone. Would you send him back in with it?"

"I'll do that." After thanking the instructor, Amy charged out the front door. What was he thinking, breaking the no-phone rule, odd as it was? And she'd been so good herself too. She bolted across the grass, ready to confront him.

She found Abel seated on a bench next to a tall and interesting abstract sculpture. He was facing away from her.

"Thank you so much," Abel said into the phone. "I look forward to it. Have a great day." Seeming to sense her approach, he turned around on the seat. Then he leaped to his feet, beaming. "I have incredible news."

10

Grace

"Is there anything I can do to help?" Grace asked as she and Winston entered the kitchen.

Charlotte stood at the counter. She was slicing carrots on a cutting board that was surrounded by mounds of vegetables. The inn usually held a wine and cheese social hour every night for guests, but this evening it had been rolled into a reception for the pottery festival and chamber of commerce. It had required expanded preparations, both in amount and number of choices offered.

Charlotte pointed at the refrigerator. "How about grating cheese? I'm making cheese puffs tonight." She grinned. "With gluten-free flour."

Grace opened the fridge and took out a block of cheese from a local farm. "You found some."

"Sure did." Charlotte continued to chop. "At Hanson's. I swung by there after the farmers market, where I bought cauliflower, carrots, and kale, all picked today so they're extremely fresh. Oh, and the last of the eggplants." She motioned to a pile. "I'm making dinner with those later this week."

"You're amazing." Grace pulled out a plate and the grater and got to work. "So, I'm dying to know what Dean wanted." Was it her imagination, or did her sister's cheeks turn pink when she said the chef's name?

"You're looking at the new judge for Brisket by the Bay," Charlotte said with a grin. "What a tough gig, huh? But I guess somebody's got to do it."

Brisket by the Bay was a contest scheduled for the last night of the pottery festival at the lakefront park. Although many people thought of pork or chicken when it came to barbecue, beef brisket had very devoted fans, with much vying as to who had created the most delectable, melt-in-your-mouth recipe.

"That's great," Grace said. "If you need any help, let me know. I love brisket any way it's made."

Winston yipped as though in agreement, making the sisters laugh. Then he flopped down on the floor with a sigh, legs spread so his belly rested on the cool floor.

They worked in silence for a few minutes, a companionable routine honed by years of practice.

"How did it go today at the building site?" Charlotte asked.

"I can't believe how fast the house is going up," Grace replied. They hadn't had a chance to talk before the design committee meeting. Afterward, Grace had taken care of some bookkeeping and double-checked the guest suites to make sure they had fresh towels and toiletries.

Since they were alone in the kitchen, she added, "As far as Dylan is concerned, it was interesting. He got to meet the Halstead family, and Evan really took a shine to him. It was the cutest thing." She explained how Evan had peppered Dylan with questions about his work as an architect.

"Evan is really bright and such a great kid," Charlotte remarked.

"He certainly is," Grace said. "Speaking of the Halsteads, I hope Kelli likes the design board."

"Me too." Charlotte began arranging cut vegetables in an attractive pattern on a platter.

"Maybe we should redecorate," Grace suggested, glancing around the room.

Charlotte rolled her eyes in mock dismay. "Oh please, not that. We've finally gotten this place perfect."

"You're right," Grace said.

In fact, the inn had been featured in magazines due to the sensitive remodeling they'd done, updating it without destroying its historic character. The inn was also the backdrop for *Comfort and Cheer from Magnolia Harbor Inn*, the cookbook Charlotte was currently working on. Grace guessed that people visiting after the book was published would expect to see the same decor.

"Besides, we're too busy," Grace said. Redecorating needed to happen in the slow season, and this year they weren't getting one. "Maybe I'll settle for repainting my bathroom." Grace lived in a suite of rooms in the mansion while Charlotte stayed in a small cottage on the property.

"Good plan. Bathrooms don't have much square footage to deal with." Charlotte consulted the printed menu in front of her. "In addition to these crudités, I'm preparing rolled-up meat and blocks of cheese with gluten-free crackers. We'll also have vegan stuffed mushrooms, antipasto skewers, and shrimp cocktail."

"Vegan stuffed mushrooms? Interesting." Grace would eat mushrooms any way Charlotte came up with. "You're amazing."

Charlotte tipped her head in acknowledgment. "Right back at you." She pulled plastic wrap over the platter to cover the vegetables. "You know, this is one of the most unusual visitor groups we've ever had. I wonder how it's all going to turn out."

"I hope with a happy ending," Grace said. "I have a feeling Dorothy Prescott really loved her grandchildren, even if they don't see that right now."

"They're all grown up." Charlotte tucked the wrap around the bottom of the platter. "If she was trying to discipline them, it's kind of late."

Grace finished grating cheese and set aside the grater. There was a satisfactory heap of cheese on the plate. The course corrections she'd made in her own life came to mind. "But not too late to change. We all make mistakes. If we're lucky, we get another chance."

11

Amy

Amy crossed her arms and scowled at her husband. "That's nice, but you're not supposed to be on the phone, remember?" She also thought it was a stupid rule, but she was doing her best to abide by it. Abel should too. It was only fair.

Abel's smile faded. "I know you're mad. But please listen." His tone was urgent. "Once I explain, you'll understand."

A familiar figure ambled along the winding path through the sculpture garden. It was Phillip.

"Hide that phone," she hissed, grabbing Abel's arm. She tilted her chin in the attorney's direction. "We've got company."

Abel stuffed the phone into his pocket and smiled as the attorney approached. "Hey, Phillip. What's up?"

The attorney regarded the couple with twinkling eyes. "I was poking around downtown in some delightful shops, and I thought I'd swing by and see how things are going with you two."

Amy felt sweat break out on her forehead. She hated being deceptive, but her darling husband had given her no choice. "Everything is great. We just finished up our lesson for today, and we'll be returning tomorrow for another." She rested her hand on Abel's arm. "Why don't you go check with Brianna about what time we should be here?"

He took the hint and trotted toward the door of the arts center.

Phillip glanced at the building's facade. "I had no idea that they had named this building after your grandmother. But she was like that—so modest. Most of her gifts were anonymous."

"It was quite a surprise." Amy could see Abel through the window, talking to Brianna. "I had to pick my jaw up off the floor when I saw it. It's such a beautiful building, and the instructor was so nice." She forced herself to stop babbling. "Anyway, we're on our way back to the inn. You?"

"After a couple more stops, yes," Phillip said. "The pottery festival reception at the inn later will be a good opportunity for you to meet some folks."

At first Amy didn't quite understand. "Oh, was Grammie involved with that too?"

"Yes, indeed." He smiled. "She helped launch the festival a number of years ago."

The front door opened, and Abel came out.

"I'll see you both later. Have a nice afternoon." Phillip continued through the garden, waving at Abel, who returned the gesture.

Once the attorney was out of earshot, Amy said, "All right, spill it." She fell into step beside her husband as they headed for the parking lot.

Abel rubbed his cheek, refusing to meet Amy's eyes. "I got an interview for a new job. It's a big step up." He dragged in a breath. "But the company is in California."

Amy jerked to a halt. "California? We live in Georgia." She had zero interest in moving. The South was her home.

Her husband looked at the blue sky, the sidewalk, a cluster of bushes, anywhere but at her face. He scratched the back of his head. "I know. But you'll be able to get something. Actually, you won't need to right away. I'll be making—"

"It's not just about the money," Amy said, cutting him off. "I love my job. I love the people. I even love my boss." *Sometimes.*

"I know. I get it. Really, I do." Abel pulled the key fob out of his pocket and clicked the button, making the car beep. "But when they headhunted me, I wanted to explore the opportunity. I was curious."

She understood. Part of the excitement of their tech careers was climbing the ladder, seeing how high they could go, especially when stock options and bonuses were offered.

Amy opened her door and climbed in. "But you didn't say a word to me about it before you applied." That was the real issue. To her dismay, she felt tears begin to burn. "How could you?"

"I'm sorry." Abel slid into the driver's seat and inserted the key. "I honestly didn't think anything would come of it."

"What else are you hiding?" Amy's throat closed, and she could hardly squeak out the words. She clenched her fists so tight that her fingernails bit into her palms.

"Come on." Abel backed the vehicle out of the parking space and drove to the exit, where he stopped. "There's nothing else. And besides, I didn't have the interview yet. I probably won't get an offer anyway."

The tears filled her eyes and spilled down her cheeks. "But you want it."

His silence told her everything she needed to know.

"Once Grammie's will goes through, neither of us will need to work." Amy shivered at the idea since she loved her career. But she wanted to remind him what was at stake with this quest they were on.

Abel appeared intent on driving so she thought he hadn't heard her, but he finally said, "I never thought much about your family's wealth. And to be honest, I don't care about it. I want to do something productive with my life. That's why I'm passionate about my career."

She had to give him points for that. Some men would gladly enjoy a free ride, but Abel had more integrity than that. She decided to let it go for now. "What do you want to do for the rest of the afternoon?"

He reached out and took her hand. "How about relaxing on our little balcony? You and me and a couple of good books?"

Amy smiled. "I saw a whole bookcase full of books at the inn. I'm sure we can find something to read."

"How was the farm?" Amy asked Savannah that evening at the reception downstairs at the inn. The sound of chatter and laughter echoed as people stood in groups or filled plates at the appetizer buffet.

Savannah frowned and leaned close to her sister. "It was gruesome. I actually fell down in the barn while cleaning the stalls. I was filthy."

Amy suppressed a giggle. Her younger sister had always been fastidious about her appearance and cleanliness. She flashed back to a memory of holding Savannah up to the sink so she could wash imaginary germs off her tiny fingers.

Savannah tossed her hair. "Go ahead and laugh. I can now. But at the time I felt like quitting and getting out of there."

"I hear you." Amy poured two glasses of red wine, then handed one to Savannah. "In fact, I know exactly what you mean. You should have seen me today at the pottery studio. What a joke."

"Going that well, is it?" Savannah patted Amy's shoulder. "Hang in there. It's only a few more days."

Dylan swaggered over to them, appearing casual but handsome in an open-necked shirt and pants. "Hey, Big and Little," he greeted his sisters, using their pet names. "How's it going?"

"I wanted to ask you that," Amy said. "What did you do today?"

Her brother groaned as he stretched. "Hard labor. Framing." His voice dropped to almost a whisper. "Way below my pay grade."

"But you're a volunteer," Savannah said. "Like me."

"I'm used to giving orders, not following them." Dylan's gaze darted around the room before landing on a newcomer in the doorway, a pretty young woman with blonde hair and freckles. "Gotta go." He strutted off to intercept her.

Savannah's eyes held a knowing expression. "Our brother seems to have a new conquest in his sights."

Watching the young woman greet Dylan with a decided lack of enthusiasm, Amy said, "I think she's on to him."

"Good for her." Savannah raised her wineglass in salute. "On another topic, I had the best time helping the new house design team pick out colors for the interior."

Amy smiled at hearing the enthusiasm in her sister's voice. "That does sound more enjoyable than cleaning stalls."

"You have no idea how true that is." Savannah slung an arm around her sister's neck. "Some of us are going out for dinner at The Tidewater later. Do you and Abel want to come?"

"Maybe." Amy scanned the crowd for Abel, spotting him near the buffet table talking to Spencer and another man. Love and anger tangled in her chest. They still hadn't resolved the idea of him taking a job in California or the way he'd applied for it without telling her.

Grace came up to them, an older woman at her side. "Julep Buckley wanted to meet you, Amy." She smiled at Savannah. "She already knows Savannah."

"I sure do," Julep said. "She worked color magic for us this afternoon."

Amy immediately liked Julep. Something about her reminded her of Grammie. Maybe it was the intelligence gleaming in Julep's eyes or the kindness in her expression. "Nice to meet you. Are you involved with the pottery festival?" she asked politely.

Grace excused herself and slipped away, as did Savannah.

Julep put a hand on Amy's forearm. "Let's sit down. I've been waiting to meet you for a long time."

They found a spot on a love seat near the windows.

Winston came trotting along. He jumped up to sit in the six inches of space between them, making them laugh.

"Did you know my grandmother?" Amy figured that was the connection. She patted Winston, who panted in delight. He was such a cutie.

Julep took a sip of white wine. "I certainly did. I have the greatest admiration for her. So many people are caught up in their own lives, but your grandmother always made time for others. And if anyone had a valid claim of being busy, it was her. After your grandfather died, she ran the business empire single-handedly. But she never forgot Magnolia Harbor."

Amy shifted in her seat, her conscience pricking. She definitely fell into the category of self-absorbed. Oh, she and Abel wrote checks to charity, but they didn't volunteer or get involved personally. She focused on the least challenging part of what Julep had said. "I understand we had ancestors here, but I never knew much about them."

Julep chuckled. "Jeremiah Prescott helped found the town. He discovered rich veins of clay and set up a pottery factory. Prescott Pottery goods were shipped back to England and were very highly regarded in their day. He made both fine porcelain and less expensive everyday dishes and containers."

"I'm sure that was a great business at the time," Amy said. Although she probably should be interested in family history, she really wasn't. Not when dealing with the present day took all her energy and then some.

"It's more than a business that's long gone," Julep chided gently. "Because of Jeremiah's vision and hard work, South Carolina built an industry that is still supporting people today. Hence our little pottery festival. Wait until you see the work that will be on display. Some of it is museum quality. Some of it will be used by families around the dinner table. But it's all worthy."

Amy sipped her wine, wondering how soon she could make her escape. She liked her grandmother's friend and didn't want to be rude to her, but she had more pressing irons in the fire. Such as what to do about her husband's potential new job.

And how to survive the rest of her time in Magnolia Harbor.

Grace

Grace was standing by the appetizer table checking over the food when Charlotte walked up.

"How's it going?" Charlotte asked.

"Quite well, I think." Grace gestured at the almost empty platters. "They ravaged those canapés like locusts."

Charlotte laughed, reaching for a cheese puff. "I wonder if anyone noticed these are gluten-free." She popped the puff into her mouth. "Want to go to The Tidewater for dinner? I guess a bunch of people besides our guests are heading over." Because of the reception, Charlotte wasn't preparing dinner for the Prescott party tonight.

"Considering the contents of my fridge, yes," Grace said. She grabbed a cheese puff too, hoping it would take the edge off her appetite. She was starving.

Spencer walked up. "I'm heading over to The Tidewater if you ladies want to join me." He looked trim and handsome in a blue dress shirt and gray slacks, with supple leather loafers.

"We were just talking about that," Grace said. Her spirits rose at the idea of spending more time with Spencer. He'd become a really good friend, someone she depended on to be in her corner. He often came over when they had an emergency too, which was really nice of him.

"I'll give you a lift," Spencer offered. He checked his watch. "When is this winding down?"

Grace observed that the crowd had thinned and now the stragglers were headed for the door in small groups. "Fifteen minutes, maybe? I need to help clean up."

Charlotte made a shooing motion. "Go on ahead. I'll clean up and meet you over there." When Grace protested, she added, "You can order for me. Dean already mentioned tonight's specials and has requested my input on the ahi tuna."

Spencer turned to Grace. "Ready, then? I'll go get the car and pull up to the front."

"Meet you outside in a jiffy." Grace wanted to run a comb through her hair and add fresh lipstick. Plus, she needed to check Winston's dishes and make sure he was all set too. He'd already had dinner and gone out, but he sometimes munched on kibble in the evening as his version of a bedtime snack.

Charlotte stacked the dishes in a bus tub, so Grace took the tub with her and headed to the kitchen.

Julep intercepted her in the doorway. "Lovely event, Grace. I think this is going to be the best pottery festival yet."

"I think so too." Missy Perkins, the chamber of commerce director, chimed in. "I wanted to say thank you for hosting tonight." She patted her red bouffant hair. "What a great kickoff."

"No problem. It was nice seeing everyone." Grace loved the fact that the small business community in Magnolia Harbor was so close-knit. They promoted and helped each other with the mutual goal of everyone doing well and supporting the town.

She said good night and made her escape, the dishes clanking. She had a friendly date tonight in one of the best restaurants in town.

The cheerful sounds of chatter, laughter, and lively background music greeted Grace and Spencer when they entered The Tidewater.

Grace's spirits rose even higher. She realized that she needed to get out more.

"Here, let me." Ever the gentleman, Spencer reached for Grace's jacket.

"Thank you." She slid out of it and allowed him to hang it up for her.

"Two for dinner?" the hostess asked, fishing a couple of tall menus out of the rack.

"Actually three," Grace said. "My sister is joining us in a little while."

The outside door opened, and Phillip and Julep entered, smiling.

Both couples exchanged surprised and delighted glances.

"I didn't know you two were eating here tonight," Grace said. What she meant was, she hadn't known that Phillip had asked Julep on a dinner date. But why not? They were around the same age and both very nice.

"Why don't you join us?" Spencer suggested. "Unless you'd rather not."

Julep and Phillip glanced at each other and must have come to some kind of silent understanding.

"That would be wonderful," Julep said.

"We'll need a table for five instead," Grace said to the hostess.

The young woman nodded, peering into the dining room and at her book before grabbing more menus. "Right this way, please."

They followed her to a table near the gas fireplace, which Grace appreciated. Not only was it cozy in this corner to fend off the autumn air, which had turned brisk, but they had the ambience of the flickering flames to enjoy. Grace took a seat by the wall. Spencer sat to her right, and Julep and Phillip sat to her left.

After passing out the menus, the hostess said, "The dinner specials tonight are ahi tuna with tomato jalapeño chutney, sturgeon with leeks and hazelnuts, and grass-fed rib eye steak with maitake mushrooms. Your server will be right with you."

"My treat," Spencer whispered to Grace after the hostess walked away. He picked up the pitcher of ice water with lemon already on the table and poured glasses for everyone.

She shook her head with a little frown, but when he insisted, she gave in. "Thanks, Spencer. Next time it's on me."

"Deal," he said. He closed the menu. "It's rib eye for me."

Grace considered the choices. "I think I'll try the sturgeon. It sounds really different."

"Dean is an excellent chef," Julep told Phillip. "Almost as good as Charlotte."

That was nice of Julep to say, since Dean had won many awards for his food. Grace smiled at the older woman. "What are you having?"

"Shrimp alfredo," Julep answered. "I love the homemade fettuccine here."

"It all sounds so good." Phillip studied the menu, making a humming sound of appreciation. "I think I'll have the rib eye too. Sometimes you're just in the mood for a good steak."

Spencer lifted his water glass in a salute. "Well said."

Grace saw the Prescott family enter the restaurant, preceded by the hostess, who seated them a couple of tables away. With them was Tabitha Douglas, the Halsteads' social worker. Considering the siblings' special diets, she wondered what they would choose to eat.

"The Prescotts are here," she said to Phillip, waving at Amy when she glanced over.

The attorney turned with a smile to greet his clients.

"They're an interesting bunch," Julep commented. She regarded the young people with amusement dancing in her eyes.

Grace thought that was an understatement.

Phillip nodded. Putting on a pair of half-glasses, he conferred with the server now standing at his elbow.

After they placed their order, Grace saw her sister winding her way toward them through the tables.

"Whew, it's busy here tonight." Charlotte sat down, opened a napkin, and put it on her lap. "Did you already order?" She held her water glass out to Spencer, who filled it.

"We did," Grace said. "I got you the tuna as requested."

"Thanks," Charlotte answered. "Dean said he doesn't think the chutney is quite right yet, and I'm supposed to find ways to improve it."

While the server brought beverages, bread, and salads, Phillip asked Julep about the town's history, a perfect subject since she was the local historian. Grace, Charlotte, and Spencer discussed the progress on the Halstead house.

"The roof's going on tomorrow," Spencer said. "Then plumbing, electrical, and HVAC will be installed. We're right on schedule."

"I'll help cater the celebration party," Charlotte volunteered. "I can't wait for the family to move in. How exciting." She lowered her voice. "Did I tell you that Dean is going to do a fund-raiser here, with all proceeds going to the project?"

"I hadn't heard that," Spencer said. "What a generous offer. And that gives us another reason to eat here." He smiled. "Not that we need one."

"That's for sure," Grace said. "It's one of the best places in town."

While talking to Spencer and Charlotte, she'd been keeping an eye on their guests. Savannah was now bopping around the room, taking photos and talking to young people seated at the bar. She was such an extrovert. In contrast, Amy and Abel were reading newspapers at the table. *The old-fashioned way to keep up with the news*, she thought with a smile. As for Dylan and Tabitha, they were deep in conversation, with Dylan doing most of the listening. From what she'd seen of the young man so far, Grace had the inkling that the reverse was usually true. Good for Tabitha.

"Here comes our food," Grace said as she spotted the server carrying a laden tray in their direction. "And there's the chef himself."

Dean often made a circuit in the dining room to see how things were and to check on guest satisfaction.

The server set the plates in front of them at the same time Dean arrived at their table.

"How is everyone tonight?" Dean asked with a disarming smile. The restaurant owner was undeniably handsome with his attractive features and impeccably maintained five-o'clock shadow.

Before anyone could answer, Savannah hurried over to Dean, phone in hand. "Can I get a picture of you with one of those meals?" She pointed at their plates.

"What are you doing?" Phillip asked. "We're getting ready to eat."

Grace inhaled the steam rising from the beautifully presented fish filet. She picked up her fork but waited, interested in hearing more from Savannah.

"I know, but it will only take five seconds," Savannah replied. To Dean, she said, "I have tons of followers. It will be a boost for this place."

Dean shrugged, still smiling. "It's up to these folks."

Charlotte pointed at the tuna, which was a gorgeous medley of color and form. "Take my plate." She gestured toward the others at the table. "Go ahead and eat."

Savannah arranged Dean in front of the nearby fireplace, holding the plate as though offering it.

Grace gratefully took the first savory bite of sturgeon. It was excellent—the ideal choice for a fall evening.

As for the Prescotts, they were making the week far from dull.

By the looks on her dinner companions' faces, she guessed they were thinking the same thing.

13

Savannah

Her alarm went off at four the next morning. Savannah groaned. Did she really have to get up so early? She'd gone to bed after midnight, energized by her evening at The Tidewater. The food had been delicious, and she'd met many great people. She'd even felt like her old self again instead of a novice farmhand with no idea what she was doing.

She opened her eyes. The room was pitch-dark, not a glimmer of light around the pulled shades. Who in the world chose to live this way? Civilized people only rose before nine if they had to.

With a grumble, Savannah reached for her phone, the sudden brightness of the screen making her squint. Then she pushed herself to a seated position and checked her social media. The pictures of Dean had tons of likes. And so did those of her in The Tidewater lobby and at the table. Of course, she'd been wearing an attractive new outfit and had tagged the designer. Maybe she could salvage her time here after all. It would soon be a forgotten blip, receding in the rearview mirror on the highway to her dreams.

The phone rang loudly, right in her hand, and she dropped it. It shrilled again, forcing her to hunt through the covers before it woke up Dylan in the next room. Who called anymore? People she knew texted or messaged. Phone calls were for emergencies.

Savannah finally located the phone. "Hello? Who is this?" She hadn't recognized the number. "This better be good."

"It's Logan. Just making sure you're up and at 'em." His voice was hoarse with sleep, which made her feel a little better. He'd chosen this ridiculous line of work, so he deserved to be tired.

Savannah sighed in annoyance. "I set my alarm, okay? You don't have to call and check up on me like I'm a kid or something."

"Point made. See you at the farm in a few." He hung up without further comment.

She stared at the phone. "Oh boy, today is going to be a good one." Sarcasm laced her tone. At least his call had fully woken her up.

Fueled by irritation, she threw back the covers and headed for the shower.

The sun still wasn't up when Savannah set off in her car toward the farm, and neither were the residents of the houses she passed, which were still shrouded in darkness. All she'd had for breakfast was a fruit-and-nut bar and a glass of water, which didn't help her mood. She hoped there would be coffee at the farm, since there hadn't been any at the inn yet.

But despite the caffeine deprivation and her general aggravation, the peace of the quiet landscape seeped into her bones as she drove. She couldn't remember the last time she'd been out and about before sunrise. It was kind of nice.

She motored through the farm gate and bumped along the drive toward the parking area. Logan's truck was already there, and lights were on in the kitchen. That would be her first stop, she decided.

A shout to come inside greeted her when she rapped on the back door. Gladys, Logan, and Roy were seated around the kitchen table.

"Help yourself to coffee," Gladys said. She pointed to a pile of fresh doughnuts on a plate. "Those are gluten-free."

"Not bad," Logan said after demolishing one in a few bites.

Savannah didn't comment on this ringing endorsement as she poured a cup of coffee. She added cream, then joined them at the table.

"What's on the agenda today? Besides cow stalls." She smiled brightly to show them that she didn't mind repeating the chore. Reaching out, she snagged a doughnut. Cinnamon sugar, she discovered when the sweetness exploded on her tongue. "These are amazing."

Gladys gestured toward her husband. "I have to take Roy to the doctor this morning, so I'd love it if you could take care of the chickens for me. They always have food and water out, so everything has to be refilled. And check for eggs in the nesting boxes."

Checking for eggs sounded enjoyable. Savannah pictured herself wandering around with a cute little basket, plucking eggs hiding in straw.

Logan's top lip lifted slightly, as if in amusement.

"What?" she asked him.

Logan leaned back in his chair, cradling his coffee mug. "Nothing. I'm sure you'll do fine." He lifted the tablecloth. "Good. I see you're wearing boots."

"What do you mean?" Savannah asked. Then she blushed. "Oh, you mean their cage is dirty." *Will I be tasked with cleaning that too?* she wondered.

He was definitely smiling now. "No, I was thinking about your toes. Chickens peck, especially when they're hungry."

Gladys snorted. "Leave her alone, Logan." She turned to Savannah. "My chickens are very friendly. They're more like pets than livestock. I pick them up and cuddle them all the time."

"Really? I didn't know you could hold chickens." Savannah couldn't quite imagine herself with a hen in her arms, though it would make a great picture. But being photographed at the farm wouldn't help her image. In fact, it would destroy everything she'd worked so hard to build. She wanted to appear sophisticated and urban—a tastemaker, not the opposite.

"Sometimes you can, if they're the nice kind," Logan said. "But it's hard to tell by looking."

Savannah rolled her eyes at his teasing, determined not to let him get to her anymore. She swallowed her coffee and finished her doughnut. "I'm ready when you are." She gritted her teeth at the thought of returning to the barn. But all she had to do was get through it, right? Without falling down again or otherwise making a fool out of herself.

"Let's go." Logan stood.

Savannah followed Logan and Roy to the barn. The cows were in their stalls, waiting patiently to be milked.

Logan set Savannah to work dispensing chunks of hay while he and Roy set up the milking machines. One by one, the cows lifted their large heads to study Savannah with long-lashed eyes. They really were pretty, for cows anyway.

Above each stall was an old-fashioned name, and she repeated each one to herself as she delivered the hay. "Bessie, Matilda, Daisy, Belinda, Dot, Cora, and Abigail."

At the end, a cow was alone in a box stall, and even Savannah could tell she was different from the others. "What's up with her?" she asked Logan when he joined her.

Logan rubbed his chin, and Savannah had the distinct feeling he was hiding a grin. "Maisie is expecting. She's due to deliver a calf anytime."

"Oh." Savannah regarded Maisie with new eyes, experiencing a surprising trickle of interest. "Do I get to see that?"

Logan patted Maisie's nose. "If you're around. Sometimes they give birth in the middle of the night." He gestured toward the cow. "Go ahead. Give her a pat."

Savannah curled her fingers, afraid to put her hand near the cow's mouth. "She won't bite me?"

"Nah. She's pretty sweet."

She reached out and touched Maisie's nose. The cow tossed her head, which made Savannah withdraw in a hurry, but not before she felt the velvety softness of Maisie's snout.

"Try again. But talk to her this time." To demonstrate, Logan cooed endearments to the cow.

To Savannah's surprise, Maisie allowed him to fondle her ears and scratch her neck too.

"They don't have fingers," Logan added, "so they like to be scratched once in a while."

Savannah knew it would be a good long while before she'd feel brave enough to get that friendly with Maisie or any cow. But she did stroke her nose again, and this time the cow stood still. Then Maisie licked her lips with a huge tongue and set to work crunching hay again.

Savannah followed Logan back along the line of stalls, feeling a little more connected to the animals now. And she couldn't wait to taste milk from this farm.

Milking didn't take long, and soon the cows were on their way out to the pasture where they'd spend the rest of the day.

Roy gave her a tour, explaining how the milk was sent to a refrigerated tank for storage until a processor picked it up. After that it was bottled and sold, with some of it sent to other local cheese makers.

"I don't get to try it?" Savannah asked, disappointed.

"You already have," Roy said. "In your coffee. We get some of the processed milk delivered to us for our own use."

Savannah decided to have a full glass later, maybe with another gluten-free doughnut.

After the stalls were clean—without mishap today—Logan escorted Savannah to the chicken coop. The large enclosure was filled with dozens of hens scrambling around and pecking at the ground.

"Gladys usually lets them roam free," he said. "But since she's not here, we'll leave them inside the fence."

"What do I do?" Savannah asked. Inside the rubber boots, her toes contracted in anticipation of beaks attacking her.

Logan pointed to metal pans in the far corner, barely visible beyond a sea of hens. "The grain needs to be refilled and the water checked. Sometimes they get it dirty or spill it. You'll have to wash and refill the water pans."

Savannah opened her mouth to protest, but then she saw the amusement lurking on Logan's face. She lifted her chin. "Show me where I can find the food."

When she entered the pen carrying a sack of grain, the chickens flocked to her with cries of excitement, but thankfully none mistook her feet for food. As soon as she filled the feeder, they attacked the grain in a frenzy, sometimes chasing each other off for a better spot.

"Now I understand the origin of the phrase *pecking order*," she mused, noticing that smaller hens were pushed aside. She sprinkled some grain for them, gratified when they got to eat before the others caught on.

"Look at the chickens. Aren't they cute?"

Savannah turned to see a young mother with two children peering into the pen, a boy and a girl about two and four years old. Logan must have opened the farm stand.

"Check out their feathers," Savannah said to the children. "There are so many different colors. Black and white and red and gray."

The little girl began to count under her breath, getting fairly high before messing up and starting over.

"There are a lot of hens, aren't there?" Savannah said. "More than I can count, since they keep moving around."

A truck marked *Hanson's Farm Fresh Foods* pulled in next to the farm stand, and a woman got out. She and Logan spoke for a moment. Then he picked up a crate of vegetables while she opened the back doors of the truck.

"You're good with the kids," the young mother said. "I'm Emily, by the way, and these two are Oliver and Anya."

Savannah gave the family a little wave. "Nice to meet you. I'm Savannah. I'm temporarily working here at the farm."

Emily pointed at her. "Hold on. I know you. You're a stylist on social media. You were in an online feature about the new fashion of the South."

"That's right." Savannah preened a little. She was still thrilled about being included as a tastemaker in her region. Next stop, New York.

To her dismay, Emily pulled out her phone and began snapping photos. "This is so great. I can't wait to share these. Savannah Prescott feeding chickens. What is this, farm chic?"

"No pictures, please." Savannah dropped the sack of grain, causing it to spill everywhere, and threw up her arms in front of her face.

The chickens went wild, squawking and flying up and pecking madly.

Savannah turned around and hunched over, trying to avoid the photos and being injured by flailing chickens. Fluttering wings hit her legs, and clawed feet climbed all over her boots.

Why had she told Emily her name? Savannah sighed. Her ego, her vanity, had gotten the best of her again.

14

Amy

When Amy gave Winnie her phone this time, it was a little easier. Everything seemed to be on track at work for a change, so she could relax and let it go.

"What should we do this morning?" Amy asked Abel. The pottery lesson wasn't until the afternoon, so the next few hours were free.

"I have an idea," Winnie said. "If you don't mind me making a suggestion."

"Of course not," Amy said. "You probably get asked about activities in the area all the time."

"We sure do." Winnie shifted her stance, holding the locked metal box against her hip. "A lot of people enjoy taking rides in the countryside. There are all kinds of interesting things to see." She paused. "And as a Prescott descendant, you might like checking out the factory ruins."

Amy's heart gave a leap. "You mean the factory Jeremiah Prescott built?"

"Yes," Winnie said. "There's not much left now, of course, but it's still a pretty spot. The county took it over for a park so there are paved paths. Some people have picnics there."

"Sounds good to me," Abel said. He glanced at Amy. "Want to check it out?"

Amy nodded.

"I'll ask Charlotte to make you a lunch," Winnie said. "And I've got a local map at the front desk. I'll mark the route." She carried the box from the dining room.

"The people here are wonderful," Amy said. Thinking of her grandmother, she felt a pang of sadness. It was too bad they hadn't come to Magnolia Harbor with her at least once during the pottery festival. It would have been nice. Maybe they would have stayed here.

Phillip entered the room and made a beeline for the coffeepot. "This is my last cup," he said with a laugh. "I promise."

"What are you up to today?" Amy asked the attorney. It must be fairly boring to sit around and watch her and her siblings work on their assignments.

Phillip dispensed coffee into his mug. "I'm going over to the building project as a volunteer." He added sugar and stirred. "I worked my way through college on a construction crew. It's been a while, but I still remember a thing or two."

"That's great," Abel said.

After breakfast, Amy and Abel went upstairs to wash up and grab jackets and gloves. The day was sunny, but a breeze was tossing the treetops. In the shady woods, it might be chilly.

She glanced at Abel, who was stuffing the outdoor clothing into a small pack. They still hadn't discussed his possible job change. He hadn't mentioned it, and Amy had been reluctant to bring up a difficult topic while they were getting along so well.

Last night at dinner, they'd chatted and laughed in a way that reminded her of the early days in their relationship. They'd borrowed the financial papers from the front desk and shared interesting articles with each other. Other people didn't get it—Savannah bluntly said they were strange—but the business world was one of their favorite topics.

Amy realized that it ran in the family. Jeremiah Prescott was an entrepreneur. He'd moved to a new land and started a company. That was courageous of him.

"I wonder if entrepreneurship is in the genes," Amy mused. "Think about it. Most of the people who came to this country were self-employed. And brave." They'd left everything familiar behind to seek their fortune in a new place. Amy didn't even want to leave Georgia.

Abel zipped the pack. "That's an interesting theory. My ancestors came over in the late 1800s and started a business in New York. So perhaps I got that gene too." Amy had met Abel at a company launch when they were both working in downtown Atlanta. "Ready?"

"I think so." Amy scanned the room to make sure she hadn't forgotten anything. "Even though we work for other people right now, we're still entrepreneurial."

"Maybe." Abel opened the room door and stood back to let her exit first. "At least in our industry we get perks for that. Stock options and so forth."

He was right, but something in Amy wondered what it would be like to be the full owner of the ideas she generated. She'd never given much thought to her inheritance, but it might offer the possibility of starting her own company. Money was the main barrier, next to having a stellar business plan, of course. She'd have to be very careful, though. She didn't want to squander the money her ancestors had worked so hard to accumulate.

Down at the front desk, a packed picnic basket awaited, along with four bottles of water and a map.

"Thank you," Amy said. "This is amazing."

Winnie beamed. "We pride ourselves on great service." She leaned on the counter, using a pen to indicate the route to the factory site.

They put the lunch and bags in the car and set off.

"Since we've got a few hours until lunch, do you want to take the long way to the park?" Abel asked when he halted the car at the end of the drive.

"Sure. It's a great day for a ride." She put on her sunglasses and sat back, ready to enjoy the journey.

After a leisurely drive, they spotted a large sign for the recreation area that read *Prescott Park*.

"I didn't know they named it after my ancestor," Amy said.

"Impressive," Abel said, veering onto the freshly paved access road. "They seem to take good care of it too."

The access road was short, and soon they came to a parking lot with only a few cars in it. Amy saw a woman and two dogs walking on a paved path. Near the path was a small building with a sheltered bulletin board next to it. Maps and documents were protected behind glass.

Since it was breezy, they put on their jackets. Abel removed their lunch from the picnic basket and stowed the food and four bottles of water in the pack.

Amy didn't have anything to carry. Then she realized something. "Oh no. I can't take photographs without my phone."

Abel picked up one last item from the picnic basket. It was a disposable camera. "Here you go. Winnie thought of everything." He tossed the package to Amy.

"I hope I can remember how to use one of these things." Amy laughed as she opened the package and removed the camera. "Stand in front of the sign."

Abel walked over to the bulletin board, where the Prescott Park sign was visible behind him, and gave Amy his best smile.

As Amy pushed the button, she hoped she was getting all the letters of the sign in the shot. As a kid, she had tended to cut people's heads off when taking their picture.

"All right," she said, joining Abel at the sign. "Which way?"

He traced a finger along the map, not touching the glass. "This path goes to the factory ruins. And this one goes around in a big loop to an overlook."

"Why don't we check out the ruins, then go up to the overlook for lunch?" Amy scanned the sky. There were only a few puffy white clouds so they'd most likely get a gorgeous view from there.

Abel snagged one of the folded maps that were available for visitors and tucked it into his jacket pocket. He shifted the pack straps to a more comfortable position and said, "Ready when you are."

"I'm ready." Amy fell into step beside Abel as they walked along the wide and level paved path.

On either side were woods, and through the trees on the right, a stream gurgled. She tried to imagine how this area had appeared a couple hundred years ago.

Dirt paths led off to the left and right, marked with small trail signs.

Abel carefully checked the map each time. Finally, he said, "This way to the factory ruins."

The winding narrow trail led through the woods, skirting boulders and fallen trees. Soon Amy noticed scattered bricks and a length of concrete pipe. "This must be it," she said.

Around the next bend, they came across a fallen-down chimney and part of a wall.

A sign on a post stated the years a factory had stood on the spot and gave some information about the owner.

"There's an old clay pit around here somewhere," Amy said. She took a few pictures of the wall, the sign, and the whole site. By studying the bricks among the ferns and leaves, she got a rough idea of the building footprint.

They pushed through the woods and located the pit nearby, now a pond filled with murky water from the clay deposits on the bottom. Most of the surface was covered with water lilies.

Amy stood on the shore, trying once again to imagine the factory up and running. In those days, the kilns would have burned wood or coal. No electricity, of course. How had they mass-produced items without machinery? This thought started her brain whirring with curiosity.

She reached for her phone to find out, but of course, her pocket was empty. "I keep forgetting I don't have my phone. I wanted to research online how they made dishes in the 1700s."

"We can research it later," Abel said. "Ready for our hike?" He wiggled his legs as though eager to get moving.

"That's right. You haven't been going on your runs," Amy said. "You must be champing at the bit to get some exercise."

Abel nodded. "I'm not going to lie. It feels good to stretch my legs." He led the way to the overlook path, which branched off the paved trail.

Amy had the sense they were circling a small but steep hill, gradually working their way upward under the shelter of the fall forest. A woodpecker knocked, and a squirrel darted up a tree.

When Amy spotted a hawk circling above them on the wind, she paused to watch, struck by awe. Her life was urban, filled with traffic and pavement and the bustle of people going about their business. The metropolitan area of Atlanta had millions of residents. Out here she and Abel were alone, the only people within earshot or sight.

Abel climbed steadily, stopping now and then to let her catch up. About halfway, according to the map, he pulled out bottles of water and they drank.

"I need to spend more time on the stair-climber," Amy said with a laugh. "My leg muscles are burning." She walked a lot, but it was mostly on level ground.

"No pain, no gain." Abel capped his empty bottle, then returned it to the pack along with Amy's. "Ready?"

She barely was, but once again she found herself climbing step by step while her fleet, strong husband practically ran up the incline. Well, at least she could be proud of herself for getting such a good workout. It might counteract the extra calories she'd been eating since arriving at the inn. Yes, it was possible to gain weight on a vegan diet, especially when delectable desserts were available.

At last they reached the overlook, a clearing at the top of a rocky cliff. The wide, flat ledge was perfect for sitting in the sun and having lunch. Abel chose a spot at the far end where they'd have some privacy even if other hikers arrived. He took off the pack and pulled out wrapped sandwiches, sweet potato chips, cookies, cut-up vegetables, and the last two bottles of water.

Amy peeked at her sandwich, gratified to find roasted portabella mushrooms, baby spinach leaves, and tomato with some kind of dressing. She wasn't a fan of look-alike food products. If she wasn't going to eat meat or cheese or eggs, then she didn't want imitations. What was the point?

Abel took a big bite of his sandwich. "This is delicious." He ate a sweet potato chip, then handed her the bag. "Try one."

Amy tasted the chips. "They're good." She sat cross-legged on the rocks, enjoying the warm sun and the light breeze. From here, she could see Lake Haven some miles away. The clay pond was below them and to their left. The countryside was a mix of woods and fields, with barns and fences clearly visible.

What a beautiful place. *My place.* The thought dropped into her mind like a pebble into a pond. Did she feel that way because Jeremiah Prescott had owned it? Maybe he'd even come up here and gazed at the view. Now her curiosity extended to learning more about her ancestor and his family. Perhaps she'd even find a portrait of him. Maybe Dylan had inherited some of his features. Or she might have.

"It's pretty nice up here," Abel remarked. "But I have to admit, I miss the city. How do people stand being so isolated?"

Startled by the contrast between his words and her thoughts, Amy laughed. She picked up the camera. "Smile. I need photographic proof of you roughing it in the woods."

Melancholy panged. Once they went home and got caught up in their busy lives, would she ever have time to visit this place again?

Grace

Grace moved about the rosebushes, clipping off the dead blossoms. Fall cleanup was always slightly sad, since it meant that the glorious summer garden was going dormant. But not for long, thankfully. Next month the camellias would bloom, and then would come saffron crocuses, Lenten roses, and daffodils. The cycle of the seasons would begin anew.

She appreciated having a little time to herself too. This week was extra busy with the pottery festival and the home-building project on top of having guests.

"But at least we're not bored," she told Winston, who was nosing around in the long grass.

A squirrel hopped across the lawn, and Winston dashed after the creature. Naturally the squirrel darted up the nearest tree, where it sat on a branch and scolded the little dog. Winston hadn't caught one yet, but he never quit trying.

Winnie walked onto the veranda, adjusting her cardigan. With a wave, she ambled across the grass. "What a nice day. I wanted to tell you that lunch is all set. The Halsteads and the committee will be here at noon."

Grace checked her watch. That gave her another hour to work before going in to help set up. "I'm excited to see their reactions to the design board. Even though it's a bit of a stretch timewise, I enjoy being on the committee."

Winnie reached out and plucked a rose, one of the last to bloom.

"What's that they always say? If you want something done, give it to a busy person?" She sniffed the rose with a smile of appreciation. "Gus went over to the building site today to help out. He's busier now than before he retired." Winnie's husband was a retired Seacoast Railway train conductor.

Retirement was something Grace didn't think about much. She saw herself running the inn well into the future. It wasn't work when you loved it, right?

"It's heartening to see the number of volunteers on this project," Grace said. "I'm proud of Magnolia Harbor and the way we come together to assist others."

"That's what it's all about, neighbors helping neighbors." Winnie glanced at the inn. "Well, I'd better get back inside. I was in the middle of some paperwork when I decided to take a break and enjoy the sunshine."

"Take as many breaks as you want," Grace said. Speaking of volunteers, Winnie had become indispensable around the inn, pitching in with all kinds of tasks. Like sorting the bills, as she was doing today. On impulse, she set down her clippers and gave Winnie a hug. "You're the best. We're so blessed to have you."

Winnie laughed as she returned the squeeze. "I feel the same way about you two. Life has been much more exciting since you came back to town."

On that pleasant note, Winnie took her leave, strolling slowly through the garden on her way back to the house.

Winston followed her, finding that more exciting than watching his mistress prune bushes. Then, as Winnie opened the door to go in, he came bolting back, chasing a falling leaf on the way.

After finishing the roses, Grace cleaned out a couple of flower beds and trimmed dead stalks and leaves.

Charlotte popped out onto the veranda. "Want coffee? I just made a pot."

Grace stood and grabbed the wheelbarrow handles. "I'll be right in after I dump this load." She trundled the barrow over to the brush pile. Then she put away her tools, took off her gardening gloves, and whistled for Winston, who was rummaging around in the bushes.

Her phone rang while she was walking into the house. Spencer. "Hey," she greeted him, continuing on her way to the kitchen. "How's it going today?"

From the background noise, she guessed he was at the construction site. "Everything is on schedule. Dylan wants to review the house plans for us, so if it's not too much of an imposition, we'll be at the inn shortly."

"Why don't you plan on having lunch here?" Grace entered the kitchen, where Charlotte was adding lettuce leaves to a platter, next to slices of tomato. After he agreed and she said goodbye, she smiled at her sister. "I hope it's okay that I invited Spencer and Dylan to join us."

"Of course. That's why I always make extra." Charlotte turned to the stove and stirred a large pot. "Guess who else is popping in? Dean. We have to decide how to score the entries in the brisket contest. Apparently the organizers are leaving it up to us."

"That should be interesting." Grace filled a mug with coffee and took a few swallows. "Let me know what I can do to help with lunch."

"How about setting out the dishes and silverware?" Charlotte suggested. "The drinks are already in there. I'm going to put this vegetable soup in a tureen and let everyone serve themselves."

"I love your homemade soup. It's just right on a fall day." Grace opened a drawer and pulled out soupspoons. "Do you want to go to town later? The pottery festival is kicking off this afternoon." There would be booths to wander through, music, and games for children.

"I do." Charlotte turned off the burner under the soup. "I put together casseroles for tonight's dinner. They're ready to go into the oven when we get back."

"You're incredible." Grace shook her head. All these extra meals meant more work for Charlotte, but she was handling it with her usual aplomb.

Charlotte laughed as she opened a closet and took out the electric soup warmer. "This is nothing compared to a restaurant kitchen on a Saturday night. Talk about a trial by fire." She set the unit on the counter. "Sometimes literally. That's why we had extinguishers handy."

Grace chuckled, then carried the dishes and silverware to the dining room.

Tabitha entered the room. She stopped and glanced around, a hand to her mouth. "I'm sorry. I guess I'm early."

"No problem. We're starting soon," Grace said. "In the meantime, help yourself to tea, sweet or unsweet." She gestured toward the pitchers. "We also have coffee and hot tea." The urns were steaming and ready.

"Thanks," the social worker said. She poured a glass of sweet tea.

"How are your folks?" Grace asked. Tabitha was about the age of her son, Jake, who now lived in Raleigh, North Carolina, and worked as a software programmer. Grace remembered Tabitha's parents from school events over the years. She recalled that Tabitha's father was a plumber and her mother did the books for the business.

"They're great. Thanks for asking. Dad is helping at the Halstead house today." Tabitha's grin was heartfelt. "It's so nice of him to take the time. He's really busy."

"Please give them my regards," Grace said.

"I will." Tabitha picked up the glass and took a sip. "This is wonderful after the morning I had. The work never stops, but I love it."

"I imagine it's a difficult job but very rewarding," Grace said.

"It definitely is. I've enjoyed spending time with the Halsteads.

They're amazing." Tabitha paused. "We could have lost them all in that fire. It was terrifying." At the memory, her face went pale.

Grace's heart was touched. She could tell that Tabitha truly cared about her clients. "I understand that it was you who suggested we build them a new home."

Now Tabitha's face flamed scarlet. "Did I? I don't remember. Anyway, it's so nice of you to help on the interior design committee. Kelli is really excited to see what you all came up with."

"I'm more than happy to do it," Grace said.

Voices drifted in from the hall.

"I love this place," Evan said excitedly. "Is it really from the 1800s? It doesn't look that old."

Tabitha smiled. "Evan is so bright. He's going to be in the gifted class at school. And Mia is also at the top of her class."

"That's fantastic," Grace said, returning her smile. "I'm glad both of them could come today."

"Me too. Fortunately, it's a half day at school."

Grace checked over the buffet table. "Please excuse me. I'm going to pop into the kitchen and tell Charlotte we're almost ready."

By the time Grace and Charlotte returned from the kitchen with the food, the whole gang had gathered. In addition to the Halsteads, Julep, Helen, Spencer, Dylan, and Phillip were attending the meeting.

"The only one missing is Savannah," Grace said to Winnie. "Have you heard from her?"

The front door opened and shut, and running footsteps thumped across the hall. "Sorry I'm late." Savannah stood in the doorway, breathless. A piece of hay clung to her long hair.

"I guess we've got everyone," Grace said.

Savannah rushed into the room and immediately began telling her brother about a pregnant cow, news he met with a bemused expression, although Tabitha seemed interested.

After Winnie said a heartfelt blessing, everyone lined up at the buffet table.

Grace and Charlotte stood back and watched to be sure everything was going smoothly. Once the guests were eating, the innkeepers and Winnie made their plates.

The vat of soup was almost empty. "This seemed to be a hit," Grace said, managing to fill three bowls with the remains.

"Good to know," Charlotte said. "I'll add it to my list of keeper recipes." She placed a second piece of wheat bread on her tall sandwich and cut it, then put half on Grace's plate.

The women joined the others, Grace seated next to Spencer. Dylan and Tabitha were across from each other, and Savannah was entertaining the Halsteads at the other end with her adventures at the farm. Grace overheard something about chickens going crazy when she spilled grain all over their pen.

"So, today is going well," Grace said to Spencer. "Glad to hear it."

Spencer set his spoon down. His bowl was almost empty. "We're right on track, according to the schedule. Phillip and I are going back this afternoon. But Dylan is going to do some work on the house plans before we finalize the doors, windows, and interior walls."

Tabitha turned to Dylan, her eyes wide. "You are? I know the Halsteads had a couple of ideas that the first architect didn't include." She lowered her voice. "I don't think they wanted to complain. They felt so grateful."

Dylan wiped his mouth with a napkin. He seemed almost bashful when he spoke. "The plans are good, but I think we can improve the layout a tweak. Make it easier for Evan to get around the house."

Grace glanced at Spencer, who lifted his brows.

As for Phillip, he was beaming between bites of his sandwich. But he didn't comment.

"That's wonderful," Tabitha said to Dylan, admiration in her voice.

Dylan shifted in his seat, a pleased smile hovering around the corners of his mouth. It appeared that he really cared about Tabitha's opinion. "No problem. Glad to help."

"Charlotte and I are going to the pottery festival later to check out the vendors," Grace said, changing the subject. "I heard there are some talented people exhibiting."

"I plan to go there too," Tabitha said. "I need to buy my mom a birthday present." She popped a chip into her mouth. "Want to join me, Dylan?"

Her casual invitation seemed to startle Dylan because he choked on his soup. After coughing a little, he said, "Sorry about that. Yes, I'd love to go."

"Meet me downtown after work." She told him the time.

Grace hid a smile. The sophisticated, self-impressed young architect was obviously falling hard for the sweet and compassionate social worker. Grace guessed that a few days ago, Dylan wouldn't have been caught dead wandering around a small-town pottery show.

Evan rolled up to Dylan in his chair. "Can I hang out with you this afternoon? They're going to talk about decorating and stuff." He made a comical face of dismay. "Not my thing."

Dylan pushed back in his chair so he could better address the boy. "Sure. I wanted to run a few things by you."

Judging by the tenderness in Tabitha's eyes as she watched Dylan and Evan interact, Grace suspected the budding romance was far from one-sided.

The Magnolia Harbor Inn was working its magic once again.

16

Savannah dashed back to the buffet table when she noticed Charlotte was starting to clean up.

"Can I please make another half sandwich before you take everything away?" she asked. "I usually only eat a half, but I'm starving." Working at the farm had given her a big appetite.

Charlotte made a sweeping gesture and stepped aside. "Please do. I'm flattered when people want seconds."

"Or thirds." Savannah winked. She quickly put together her sandwich. "Thanks for getting gluten-free bread. I like to have my daily carb allotment."

"Those cookies are gluten-free too," Charlotte pointed out. Several types of cookies were arranged attractively on a circular platter.

Savannah snagged a couple of chocolate chip cookies and tucked them in a napkin for dessert. "Thanks so much." She buzzed back to the table, where only the committee members were left. Her brother was working in the music room with Evan at his side.

As Savannah scooted her chair up to the table, she caught Mia's eye.

The shy teen's gaze immediately dropped. But then Mia mumbled, "I follow you on social media."

"You do?" Savannah asked. Apparently she had followers everywhere, even in this tiny town in the middle of nowhere. It was a humbling thought. "Did you like the red boots or the black ones better?" Savannah had modeled two new styles of boots recently, her last real posts before being exiled.

Mia sipped her tea, thinking. "It's hard to decide. The red ones are cute, but they kind of take over your outfit, if you know what I mean. While the black ones, they're just cool and go with everything."

Seeing a wistful expression in the teen's eyes, Savannah asked, "What size do you wear?" Mia was about her height, and it turned out they wore the same size shoes. "Tell you what. I've got those black boots in my car. You can have them."

Mia gasped loudly, attracting the attention of her mother and grandmother, who were chatting with Grace and the other ladies. "Seriously?" Mia bounced up and down. "That would be great."

"I'd like to give Mia a pair of boots, if that's okay," Savannah said to Kelli. "People send me merchandise all the time so I'll promote it."

"I don't know," Kelli said.

"I give away a lot of stuff," Savannah said. "Ask my sister." Of course, Amy was too buttoned-up and conservative to wear the things Savannah gave her. But that was another story altogether.

"I guess that sounds okay," Kelli said. "But I want to see them first."

"Mom," Mia protested.

Savannah took a bite of her sandwich. "I'll run out and get them now."

"When you return, we'll begin the meeting," Grace said. "Everyone, get refills of coffee or tea. I'll fetch the design boards."

Savannah rushed through the foyer, pausing to spy on Dylan and Evan in the music room. Her brother was explaining what the different symbols on the blueprints meant, and Evan was listening intently.

Evan suddenly gave a barking cough.

"Do you need some water?" Dylan asked. "I'll crack one of these bottles open for you."

"Thanks," Evan replied, his voice husky.

Savannah couldn't believe it. Her brother hadn't been so nurturing since when? Maybe when she'd been small. She remembered him getting her snacks and helping her with her boots, that kind of thing. Shaking her head, she opened the front door and slipped out.

She rooted through her trunk that was crammed with luggage and boxes and finally found the boots. They normally cost more than three hundred dollars, but she wasn't going to mention the price. That would probably make Mia afraid to wear them, and they should be enjoyed.

When Savannah returned to the dining room, the shoebox under her arm, Grace was setting a revised design board on an easel so everyone could see it.

"Savannah, do you want to give the presentation?" Grace asked. To the others she said, "Savannah took the designs from good to great. She has a wonderful eye and sense of color."

The others applauded as Savannah handed Kelli the shoebox, then took her place at the easel. "Thanks, everyone. But let's not forget something important here. The committee came up with this, and I just added the finishing touches." She began to clap. "So let's give them a hand."

The open area of the downtown park was filled with small white tents, except for a spot near the water where a band was playing and children were dancing.

Savannah headed for the first row of booths, planning to work her way systematically through the vendors. Aromas of grilling meat and popcorn drifted her way, making her stomach rumble despite the fact she'd had lunch only a couple of hours ago. Thanks to all the physical labor, her appetite was out of control.

Most of the tents sheltered displays of pottery from the rustic to the refined. Savannah was impressed by the range of talent and creativity. She examined a brown clay mug embossed with a scowling face complete with blue marble eyes and white squares for front teeth. She didn't know whether to laugh or be horrified.

"How would you like to wake up to that?" someone asked.

Savannah whirled around. Logan was standing next to her elbow, wearing an amused expression. "Well, it does express how I feel in the morning." Before he could respond, she warned him with a shake of her finger. "Don't say it."

Logan rubbed his chin with the back of his hand, but she wasn't fooled. He was holding back laughter.

Finally, she gave in. "Yeah, I'm not a morning person. I admit it. Is that out of the way now?"

"I haven't always been one," he said. "But I've learned to be. Farming requires it."

Without discussing it, they began ambling down the midway together, checking out the booths.

Savannah stopped to admire some mugs in shades of blue and green. They reminded her of the lake. She picked up a mug and noticed how well it fit in her hand. "I'm getting this one."

After she paid for the mug, they kept going.

"So why did you leave the big city for the country?" Savannah asked, remembering he was originally from Charlotte.

Logan was silent for a few moments, seeming to gather his thoughts. "It wasn't a sudden decision. My great-grandparents owned a farm, and my grandmother used to talk about what it was like growing up there. Boy, did she have a green thumb. Her vegetable garden had to be an acre at least, and she also grew flowers. Her garden was like paradise."

By the glow on his face, Savannah assumed he'd been especially close to his grandmother. She felt a pang of sorrow for her own grandma. How much more could she have learned from Grammie? Savannah had taken her for granted and barely listened to her stories. Like this festival, for example. Her ancestors had a factory that made dishes, and Grammie had honored that history by supporting potters in this generation.

"I used to help my grandma in the garden," Logan continued. "She taught me a lot."

"So she inspired you to start a farm?" Savannah realized she wanted to hear more. She was starting to like Logan, now that he had set aside his superior attitude.

"Yeah, I'll say she did." Logan halted, and other festivalgoers diverted around them. "While I was away at college, I got interested in the local food movement. Small farms are making a comeback, and when I realized I could be one of them, I knew I had found my passion."

"I've found mine too," Savannah said. "It started with making doll clothes, believe it or not." She thought back to those early days when she'd cut up discarded clothing to make little outfits, mostly by hand, since the pieces were so small. "I discovered that the right clothing makes a big difference in how you feel." She stood up straighter, knowing that her clogs, strategically faded jeans, and fitted leather jacket were perfect for this occasion.

Logan lifted his brows, a mocking light in his eyes. "And how do you feel in muck boots and overalls?"

With a burst of laughter, Savannah cuffed his arm. "You are so . . . so . . ." She couldn't think of a suitable word. "Infuriating. That's it."

He ducked away, laughing. "That's what they tell me." Then he sobered. "Actually, I think you're doing a great job at the farm. I know it's all new to you."

"Yeah, it's growing on me," Savannah admitted as they began walking again.

"You should have seen me the first couple of seasons," Logan said. "I had no idea what I was doing. But since I loved it, I kept trying." He sent her a sideways glance. "And now my veggies are sold in gourmet grocery stores in Charleston."

Savannah's mouth dropped open. "That's wonderful. Designer vegetables. Who would have thought? So, what's your farm called?"

"Rock Bottom," Logan answered. "I'm in a little valley near a stream, and I was starting from the bottom."

She took her phone out of her purse and began to search for his farm.

"I'm not on social media," he said, "so don't bother checking."

"What?" Savannah stared up at him, aghast. "How are people supposed to find you if you're not on social media? Every business should have an online presence."

"Maybe you can help me with that," Logan replied. "I'd like to add online ordering for my customers. They've been asking about it."

"I can definitely help you. I'm really good at creating an image and media campaigns. That's what I did for myself." She located her most popular page. "See?"

He took the phone and studied the photographs she'd posted. "A lot of people like you. Why exactly do you do this?"

As they walked through the park, working their way toward the music, Savannah explained her business model to Logan.

"So you don't actually have to make or sell anything yourself," Logan concluded. "You just advertise other people's stuff and you get paid." He sounded astonished.

"Yes, I make a commission when people buy what I promote," she said. "I'm also aiming to get officially hired by a couple of designers as a brand ambassador."

Logan scratched the back of his neck. "I guess I've been in the country too long. I've never heard of that."

"Most people haven't." Savannah held her head up with pride. She was in the forefront of an exciting new world—and making money at it. But then she stole another glance at the good-looking young farmer. He was on the cutting edge too, with his locally grown vegetables. She truly respected that.

"Do you want something to drink?" Logan asked. "There's a mulled cider stand over there."

"I'd love some cider," Savannah said. As she glanced around, she spotted her sister and brother-in-law sitting at a picnic table. "After we get our drinks, I want you to meet a couple of people."

With big, steaming cups of cinnamon-scented cider in hand, Savannah and Logan joined the couple at the table. Savannah introduced Logan and mentioned his farm.

Abel and Logan immediately began talking about sports.

"How do guys do that?" Amy asked Savannah. "They've known each other for what, two minutes?"

"Less." Savannah sipped the hot cider, which was heavenly. "How's your day going?"

Amy told her about their picnic at the park. "When we got back to town, we had another pottery lesson, then came over here to walk around." She reached for a paper bag with handles. "Want to see what I bought?"

"I got something too," Savannah said. She opened her bag and unwrapped the mug, which was swaddled in tissue.

"Oh my, I don't believe it." Amy put a hand to her mouth. The sisters had bought mugs from the same vendor. Amy's had a little more green on it, but otherwise they were identical.

"Great minds think alike," Savannah said with a shrug. She rewrapped her mug in the tissue and set it gently into the bag again. She flicked through her phone and checked her messages. Nothing important.

"Want a snack, Amy?" Abel rose from the bench. "There's a vegan booth over there."

"Sure," Amy said. "Something light. I understand we're having dinner at the inn later."

"Do you want something, Savannah?" Logan asked. "I kind of have my eye on a corn dog."

Savannah laughed. "I can't have a corn dog. But maybe bacon on a stick?" She reached for her wallet, but he waved off her offer of money.

"Logan seems like a nice guy," Amy said as they watched the two men walk away, chatting. "Where did you meet him?"

"Get this," Savannah said, with a roll of her eyes. "In Roy's cow barn. Logan taught me how to clean the stalls and feed the chickens." She thought back. "Well, actually we had a run-in at the farm store when I was buying my boots and overalls before that. It seems like ages ago."

"You're glowing," Amy said. Her tone held an edge of accusation. "You have a crush on him, don't you?"

Savannah considered. She really liked Logan. In fact, she felt happy being around him. She held up her hand, forefinger and thumb about an inch apart. "Maybe a tiny one." She sipped her cider. "I'm not sure yet. It's too soon."

"Be careful," Amy muttered. "You'll be leaving before long, and Logan can't exactly pick up and follow you, can he? Not if he owns a farm."

That was true, but Savannah didn't want to think about that right now. She was having too much fun. She reached for her phone again, thinking she'd take a few shots of the festival.

But her phone wasn't there. Amy had it in her hand and was sprinting toward the lake.

Amy

Shame washed over Amy in hot waves. Had she really snatched Savannah's phone and run away with it? But that remorse didn't stop her from signing into her work e-mail. All day a tickle of unease had lingered in the back of her mind. A critical meeting was scheduled for today, and she wanted—no, needed—to learn the results.

She ignored the hundred e-mails that could wait and focused on the ones regarding the meeting. Dismay grew as she read. A coworker, one she regarded as a rival due to his passive-aggressive tactics and constant nipping at her heels, was now in charge until she returned. But she knew that once her control had been relinquished, it would be almost impossible to get back. Worst of all, this project was her baby, a concept she'd dreamed up. Literally, in her sleep.

"What are you doing?" Savannah stood with her hands on her hips. "I can't believe you stole my phone."

"Sorry," Amy muttered, composing a reply, her fingers shaking. She misspelled a word and had to correct it. Then autocorrect kicked in and said something absurd. Why did this always happen when she was in a hurry?

As her sister continued to stare at her, Amy finally gave up. She needed to give some thought to her response, not fly off the handle. Of course, waiting until tomorrow would only give her coworker more time to cement his position.

"What's so important?" Savannah asked. "The guys are bringing us our food. They're going to wonder what you're doing over here, lurking under a tree."

Amy exited her e-mail and handed Savannah the phone. "Sorry. I'm having a work problem. I couldn't stand waiting until tomorrow to find out what was going on."

Savannah gave her a sympathetic look. "Is it a big deal? It must be hard being away and feeling disconnected."

"Yes, that's exactly it." Amy drew in a ragged breath. "With that job, I never have any real downtime. They expect us to be available 24-7."

"That's awful." Savannah frowned. "Everyone needs downtime to relax and recharge. No wonder you're so edgy."

Feeling chided, Amy retorted, "What about you? You post constantly. Do you ever shut your phone off?"

Savannah stared down at the phone. "I guess you're right. But at least I like what I do." She slipped the phone into her pocket. "Besides, I don't use it at the farm."

Amy barely heard this last comment. What Savannah had said struck her. Did she like her job? Oh, the challenge was energizing, and beating their competitors was thrilling at times. Creating new and better programs was also rewarding and sometimes even enjoyable.

But did she like it? Like a bell tolling, the answer chimed in her mind. *No.*

Struck by this truth, Amy stopped dead.

"Are you coming?" Savannah was now walking backward.

"Yes, I'll be right there," Amy promised. Sighing, she realized that she couldn't ignore her insight. She didn't like her job, but it controlled her to the point of acting like a child. What was she going to do about it?

Her mind whirled as she walked to the picnic table.

"I got you a black bean burrito," Abel said. "A small one." He picked up his burrito and bit into it.

"Thanks." Amy slid onto the bench. She took a deep breath, trying to release her burdens. What counted right now was spending time with her husband, her sister, and Logan.

And enjoying what turned out to be an extremely tasty snack.

The next morning at breakfast, Winnie arrived with the lockbox containing their phones.

"Thanks, but I don't want to check my phone," Amy said, surprising herself. Feeling surprisingly light and free, she added, "I want a day without electronics."

Abel gaped at her. "That's different." He retrieved his phone and turned it on. "I need to see a few things."

"Go right ahead," Amy said, spooning another serving of fruit salad onto her plate.

The weather was cloudy with the threat of rain, so she decided to spend some time at the pottery studio. And maybe the library too.

Now that she had a little more room in her brain—the space where obsession about her job used to live—ideas were beginning to percolate. She knew that creative tingle well, although in the past, it had purely been related to her job. These ideas were for her. She couldn't suppress a giggle. Being self-indulgent for a change was exhilarating.

Abel studied her as he set his phone down. He cleared his throat. "About that interview . . ." He allowed his voice to trail off.

The giggles immediately fled, along with much of her buoyant mood. "What about it?" Amy stabbed a strawberry and popped it into her mouth, barely tasting the sweet juice.

He fiddled with his mug, turning it around and around on the tabletop. "Should I do it or not?"

Amy sighed, knowing the only answer she could give. "Go ahead. An interview is not an offer. And if you get one, we'll cross that bridge together."

Under the table, she crossed her fingers. She didn't want Abel to get a job offer, which was terrible of her. But she didn't want to uproot their life and move to the West Coast, although it would get her away from the job she disliked. But she disliked the thought of leaving the people and places she knew even more.

Relief shone in Abel's eyes. "Thanks for understanding. I knew I could count on you." He picked up the phone and began working the screen. "I'll send a note right now. The first interview will be by phone, so I can do it here."

"By phone? When?" But Amy had a nagging feeling she knew.

"Later this morning." Abel smiled. "I'll have to give the pottery studio a miss, if that's okay. I need to prepare for this." He squared his shoulders. "It's big."

Amy forced a smile. "Well, then, it's good I'll be out of your way. I'll be at the studio if you need me. And then poking around downtown."

"Enjoy yourself," Abel said. "See you later."

"That you will." Amy finished her fruit salad, then pushed back from the table and gathered her dishes.

At least now she'd be able to focus on her pottery and her alone time without any guilt. With her new resolve to live more lightly, she decided to have a great day, even if she was alone for most of it.

At the studio, Brianna gave Amy a lesson in throwing clay. Really it was more like spinning clay, since the method formed chunks of clay on a wheel spun by a potter's feet.

"You can go as slow or as fast as you like," Brianna said. "Watch." She demonstrated, turning a formless shape into a lovely vase in what seemed like seconds.

Amazed by Brianna's skill, Amy couldn't help but think the transformation of something rather unattractive into an object of beauty was almost a miracle of sorts. A little spark lit in her heart, the place where her creativity lived. She was no stranger to turning an idea into reality. This was just more physical and hands-on.

Brianna cut the vase off the wheel with a wire held in both hands and placed it on the table. "I suggest you start with something smaller. Maybe a mug." She handed the cutter to Amy. "Go ahead and cut off a chunk of clay."

Amy sliced off a neat rectangle and wedged it as Brianna had taught her. Wedging was kneading the clay so it would be pliable and free of air pockets and small hard spots. Then she set the blob on the wheel and perched on the seat, ready to begin.

"If you don't like how it looks, feel free to smoosh it down and start over," Brianna reminded her. "Clay is forgiving that way."

"I'll be smooshing a lot," Amy said with a laugh. Using wet hands to shape the clay, she set to work. At first she played, seeing how the pressure of her hands or fingers shaped the clay into various objects. She made a tall cylinder, then pushed it back into a blob. She formed the cup wide and shallow, like a bowl.

After an hour of messing around, Amy had a credible mug. So she made a second, figuring that she and Abel could use them for coffee, and added handles of twisted clay. She pulled out the tool Winnie had given her and used it to draw a design of loops and swirls.

At the last minute, she added a *P* to honor Prescott Pottery.

The door opened, and Brianna entered. "How's it going?"

"Great," Amy said, smiling. "I've got two mugs. They're a little deformed, but I'd like to fire and glaze them anyway. As mementos."

Brianna inspected her work. "Not bad. We'll candle them in the kiln to dry, then fire them." She put the mugs with a tray of other work ready to be dried at the low, slow heat the kiln would provide. This was much faster than air-drying, which could take days or weeks, depending on the clay and the level of humidity.

"I can't wait to see how they come out." Amy gazed upon her mugs with pride.

After thanking Brianna for her help, Amy left the studio.

Next stop was the library to learn more about Jeremiah Prescott.

Amy parked on the street near the Heritage Library, which was on Willow Street, one block over from Main. The brick two-story library was charming, with arched windows and marble steps. A metal sign on the lawn proudly announced it was built through the generosity of philanthropist Andrew Carnegie.

With a sense of anticipation, Amy climbed the steps to the entrance. She had fond memories of going to the local library with her mother and later with her grandmother after her mother died.

Inside the library, an older woman with short gray hair and a welcoming smile sat behind a semicircular desk.

"How may I help you?" the librarian asked as Amy approached the desk.

"I'm here to do some research," Amy said, shifting the tote that held her tablet and a notebook. "My ancestor was Jeremiah Prescott."

"You must be one of Dorothy Prescott's granddaughters." The woman smiled and held out a hand. "I'm Phyllis Gendel. How nice to meet you."

"Yes, I'm Amy Butler. It's nice to meet you too." She shook the librarian's hand, marveling that yet another person knew Grammie. "How did you know my grandmother?"

"She donated some family papers regarding the pottery factory to the library," Phyllis explained. "Come with me, and I'll show you."

"Great," Amy said. "Thank you."

They walked through the main library to a smaller room in the back.

"This is our history room, where we also keep rare documents." Phyllis used a key on a wrist loop to unlock the door. After switching on the light, she gestured for Amy to enter. "We keep it climate controlled in order to preserve the older materials."

Amy nodded as she scanned the metal shelves holding books and storage boxes, file cabinets, a microfilm station, and a long table for study.

Phyllis went to a glass case and used another key to unlock it. Along with a stack of precious papers, she retrieved several books about the history of the pottery. She carried the materials to the table and set them down. "I'll leave you to it. Let me know if you need anything." Phyllis slipped back out of the room.

Amy sat down at the table. The documents were kept in archival plastic sleeves. The paper had aged to a creamy ivory, and the iron gall ink had faded to brown.

She leafed through invoices, receipts, and lists of expenditures and sales. While she read, she pictured Jeremiah hunched over his work, using a quill pen. The sense of industry and pride somehow came through the documents, especially those stamped with the company name and logo, two intertwining capital *P*'s. It was quite elegant and somehow familiar.

Then she remembered a teapot her grandmother had kept in a glass case. As a child, Amy had loved its form of a kneeling camel, complete with a howdah—the basket people rode in. She'd never been allowed to handle the teapot, but Grammie had showed her the bottom and the intertwined *P*'s pressed into the ceramic, the factory mark. The teapot had been made in this factory, she realized. What a precious object. They should donate it to a museum, where it could be preserved and enjoyed by many.

While Amy browsed through the materials, she jotted down anything of interest. She also used her tablet to take pictures of the antique documents so she could show Abel and her siblings. As she was playing with the small computer, a temptation swept over her. She could sign in and get her e-mail, using the tablet.

For a long moment, she sat with the tablet gripped in her hands, warring with her conscience. She'd already slipped up once. Shame washed over her once more as she recalled how she'd run away with Savannah's phone like a naughty child with a stolen cookie.

In a decisive move, she shut the tablet off. She wasn't going to betray Grammie—or herself—again.

Amy replaced the materials inside the glass case. Phyllis would lock it when she left.

She toyed with the idea of getting lunch at the Dragonfly Coffee Shop, but another thought nudged her. The plane crash that killed her parents was covered in old newspapers, now on microfilm. Maybe it was time to put that past to rest. She'd never wanted to read about the event, but in the back of her mind she knew she was haunted by it. For example, she tended to shut down when she had to confront someone, such as her husband. She knew that behavior was tied to a child-formed belief that if she disagreed with someone, she would lose that person, just as her parents had lost each other after their fight.

Amy went over to a file cabinet and found boxes holding issues of the Atlanta paper. After locating the right year, she sat at the microfilm machine and threaded the roll. Then she scrolled to the exact date.

What she read turned all her preconceptions and false beliefs upside down. The accident had nothing to do with her parents fighting before they left. Another pilot had been flying the craft, and they'd been caught in a sudden storm. It was a tragic accident, but it had nothing to do with her parents' difficult relationship.

Amy pushed back from the desk, the burden she had carried for years lifting off her, leaving her feeling free and alive.

18

Grace

Grace and Charlotte spent the morning freshening the guest rooms, supplying new towels and making the beds. Then they joined Winnie for a coffee break in the kitchen.

"What's on your agenda for the rest of the day?" Grace asked Charlotte.

The trio sat on stools at the island while Winston napped in a patch of sunlight nearby, exhausted after following them around the house.

"I'm testing some recipes with gluten-free flour," Charlotte said. "I might include a couple in my new cookbook. Or, alternately, I can give gluten-free instructions for the baked goods."

"That's a great idea," Winnie said. "I know a lot of people have that issue."

Grace hopped off her stool to fetch the coffee carafe. "How is gluten-free flour different?" She was content to follow a recipe, trusting the person who wrote it. But professional chefs like Charlotte went beyond techniques to the science of baking.

Charlotte held out her mug for a refill. "Gluten is found in wheat, barley, and rye. But the substitutes for those, often rice flour, don't act quite the same. I've been learning that adjustments to the recipes can help with texture."

"Always something to learn, right?" Winnie said. "That's what keeps you young."

"More coffee?" Grace asked her aunt.

"No thanks," Winnie said. "Are you still going to House to Home this morning? If so, I'd love to ride along."

House to Home, located next to Hanson's Farm Fresh Foods, offered a range of interior decorating supplies, window treatments, and flooring.

Grace nodded. "I'm going to order the paint and flooring for the Halstead house." Kelli had loved the design concepts so this was the committee's next task.

"That sounds like fun," Charlotte said. She slid off the stool. "Winston and I will be baking."

Winston lifted his head and barked.

"That dog doesn't miss a trick," Winnie said. "After we go to the store, can we swing by the construction site? It would be nice to see their progress."

"Absolutely. I was planning on it." Grace rinsed her cup at the sink. "The women from church are bringing lunch today too."

"Now I'm envious," Charlotte said. "Those ladies sure can cook."

Grace agreed. The women from the Fellowship Christian Church put on legendary dinners featuring Southern home cooking.

A dreamy expression came over Charlotte's face.

"Did you just get a cookbook idea?" Grace asked, recognizing her sister's expression.

"Maybe," Charlotte murmured.

"Be sure to take notes. But remember, you're under deadline for this one." Grace referred to *Comfort and Cheer from Magnolia Harbor Inn*, the cookbook Charlotte was currently working on.

"I know," Charlotte responded. "But what do you think of a church supper cookbook? We could compile recipes and sell it as a fund-raiser."

"I'll help," Winnie said. "Some of Gus's favorite meals are recipes passed down by aunts and grandmothers." She rinsed her mug too. "Next to yours, of course, Charlotte."

"Sweet of you to say that." Charlotte gave her aunt a hug. "But I find it fascinating how recipes are passed down from generation to generation, I don't want them to be lost."

Her sister's comment made Grace realize something, "Not to change the subject, but I think that's why Dorothy Prescott had her grandchildren come here. Because of Prescott Pottery."

"I agree," Winnie said. "Dorothy's support of local potters gave her the opportunity to honor her ancestor. By the way, have you stopped by the pottery show yet?"

"We did." Grace smiled as she opened a cupboard door. "Look at this." She held out a mug with a face on it for Winnie to inspect. "I couldn't resist it."

Winnie burst into laughter. "I have to get one for Gus. It's hilarious."

"Since we're showing off purchases, check out what I bought." Charlotte displayed a gorgeous platter streaked with blue, green, and gold.

Winnie exclaimed in delight.

Then Grace glanced at the clock. "We'd better hit the road, Winnie." She bent to pat Winston. "Be good for Charlotte, you hear?"

The dog wagged his tail in response, then licked his lips.

Grace laughed and turned to her sister. "I think he associates you with treats."

Charlotte gave a sheepish shrug. "Well, I do give him a few when you're not around."

When Grace and Winnie entered House to Home, the bells above the door jingling, the owner hurried to greet them. "Good morning, ladies. How may I help you?" Rich Chambers was in his sixties, with a full head of white hair and a keen design sense. He and his wife, Mamie, had started the business decades ago.

Grace glanced around the sumptuous displays of carpet, tile, and blinds, sighing with happiness as she took them in. She loved this store. "We're shopping for the Halstead project. Have you heard about it?"

Rich stood with his hands clasped behind his back and nodded. "Through the chamber of commerce newsletter. Mamie and I want to do our part." He paused. "So we're giving you a discount. Everything at cost."

Grace couldn't hold back a gasp. "Thank you. That's incredibly generous. But we didn't expect a discount." As a business owner, she understood that local vendors had overhead and payroll to cover.

Rich reached out to touch a pile of richly colored wool rugs, his pale cheeks coloring with embarrassment. "It's the least we can do. People helped us when we were a young family. So we're passing it on."

Realizing that he didn't want her to make a fuss, Grace moved on. She pulled a piece of paper out of her tote. "Now, where should we start? I've got a list of paint colors we need. We're also searching for floors. Carpet, laminate, and tile."

"Have you seen the new laminates?" Rich led the way deeper into the store. "They hold up well under traffic and are very easy to care for. They're made for a busy family."

Grace smiled at Winnie. "Let the fun begin."

After an hour spent drawing up the order, which would be delivered to the new house by the shop as needed, Grace and Winnie headed out to the parking lot.

As Grace was unlocking the car, she noticed Kelli trotting out of Hanson's Farm Fresh Foods next door. "There's Kelli," she said.

Both Grace and Winnie waved, but Kelli didn't appear to see them. She hopped into her van and raced away.

"That was odd," Winnie said. "I hope there isn't something wrong."

"Maybe she's late for an appointment." Grace remembered the days of running around trying to meet her son's needs. There always seemed to be somewhere to go, and her to-do list never got any shorter.

When they arrived at the construction site, the sound of air guns and hammers from the roofing and exterior sheathing crews greeted them. Grace spotted Spencer and Dylan, both laying shingles as fast as they were handed to them. Under the shade of a tree, Julep and Helen were setting a long table with disposable cups, paper plates, and the like.

Grace and Winnie walked over to Julep and Helen.

"Just in time. The food is due to arrive any minute." Julep pointed to several more folded tables and chairs. "Can you help set those up? The church let us borrow them. We're having a sit-down lunch for a change."

"It sounds nice," Winnie said.

Grace and Winnie picked up the first table and extended the legs, careful to put it on a level spot. Then they moved to the next table and did the same.

On the roof, a man sang out a line from a gospel song, and others soon joined him.

The beauty of the mingled voices sent a chill down Grace's spine. "I didn't expect to hear the men's choir today," she commented to Winnie. They sang in such beautiful harmony at church. Even Glen Abrams, the pastor, was lending a hand today.

Winnie shaded her eyes with her hand and gazed up at the men. "Me either. And do they ever sound good."

They finished setting up the tables and chairs to the warm sounds of the men's voices punctuated by tools.

Other vehicles began to arrive, and women carted platters of sandwiches and slow cookers full of soups and stews over to the buffet table.

Penny Abrams, Glen's wife and a transplant from England, was among them. She'd brought a big bowl of trifle for dessert.

"This is lovely," Penny said to Grace, tucking a strand of shoulder-length blonde hair behind her ear. "Glen is enjoying the time away from his desk," she added with a laugh. The pastor could usually be found either working on a sermon or counseling members of the congregation.

"I'm overwhelmed at this outpouring of community support," Grace said. "We've had volunteers from all kinds of groups. And guess what? Rich Chambers gave us a huge discount on the paint and flooring." Grace planned to tell everyone about the business owner's generosity. She knew it would garner him goodwill, even if he already had plenty of that.

"How generous," Penny said. "Kelli was saying that she wants to throw a big housewarming party to thank everyone."

"We can do that," Grace said, her mind already whirring with ideas.

Spencer blew a whistle to signal lunch, and the crews swarmed from their stations over to the lunch area.

Glen gave a blessing, and then lines formed at the food table.

Spencer hung back with Dylan.

Grace went over to say hello. "You're making some major progress today," she remarked as she studied the building.

"We certainly are," Spencer said. "Once we get the roof and exterior walls finished, we'll put in the windows and doors. Then on to the inside."

Dylan smiled as he regarded their work. "I've forgotten how much fun it is to be part of a crew. When I was in college, I used to do construction during summer breaks." Casually dressed in a T-shirt, jeans, and work boots, he seemed right at home.

The urbane, cynical young man who had arrived at Grace's inn mere days ago was nowhere in sight.

Phillip, who was chatting with Julep but kept glancing over, appeared pleased with Dylan's transformation.

Now and then Dylan craned his neck toward the street, and soon Grace saw why. A familiar sedan pulled up, and Tabitha hopped out. She waved at Dylan, and he excused himself to greet the social worker.

Grace watched as the pair began talking with animation, wandering over to the house so Dylan could point out various aspects of the job.

Most people were through the line.

"Want to grab a bite?" Spencer said. At Grace's assent, he ushered her toward the table.

Grace took a spoonful from several of the slow cookers—macaroni and cheese, chili, and chicken stew with black olives and tomatillos. She didn't care if the food got mingled on her plate. That was the pleasure of potluck. After grabbing a fresh homemade roll, a pat of butter, and a glass of sweet tea, she was all set.

She and Spencer sat down at the end of a table. Some of the crew had already finished the main course and were enjoying dessert. Others had taken cookies and brownies with them back to the work site, where they talked in groups.

"This is so good," Grace said between mouthfuls. She couldn't decide which dish she liked best. "Charlotte wants to collect local recipes for a fund-raiser," she said to Penny.

"What a great idea," the pastor's wife said. "We have the best church suppers. We might as well share the wealth."

"I vote yes for that," Glen said, joining them at the table. When his wife eyed his heaped plate with amusement, he added, "I forgot how hungry physical labor makes you." In his early sixties, the pastor was wiry and fit. He claimed his busy congregation kept him young.

"Save room for my trifle," Penny said.

"Don't worry," Glen said. "Hopefully there will be some left." The big bowl was already almost empty, since her signature dessert was well-known. He grinned at his wife. "If not, you can make me my own batch."

"You'll be lucky," Penny said with twinkling eyes.

"Oh, but I am," her husband replied. Glen and Penny had four grown children and half a dozen grandchildren, but they often acted like newlyweds.

Glen's phone chimed, and he dug it out of his pocket. "Sorry, but you never know . . ." He read the text, concern growing in his eyes. "Evan Halstead was admitted to the hospital. He has pneumonia."

Savannah

Savannah drove through the farm gate with anticipation singing in her heart. What a change from a couple of days ago. She was part of the farm now, and she felt connected to Roy and Gladys, the cows, and yes, even the chickens. As for Logan . . . her heart gave a traitorous lurch. She had to admit that she liked Logan. A lot.

She parked next to his truck. Now that she knew more about his own farm and his goals, she admired the way he was helping Roy. It didn't make his own work go away, so he had to check his gardens and hoop houses before coming over here and then race back in the afternoon to do his chores. The only saving grace was that the main growing season had passed, and he was mostly harvesting kale and potatoes.

Savannah popped into the house to grab a cup of coffee and say hello to Gladys. Then it was out to the barn, mug in hand, to help. The men were finishing up the milking. Was it her imagination, or was the smile Logan directed at her extra bright?

"Good morning," she said. "How's it going?"

"Just fine," Roy said. He still stood with a crutch, but he was checking the milk lines. "We'll be out of your way in a few minutes."

Savannah went down the line, patting the cows and greeting them. She was getting to know each distinctive face and personality. Bessie was a sweet old gal, and Dot was leery of being patted. Savannah always tried anyway. This time her fingers grazed Dot's nose before the animal jerked away.

"She's a shy one," Logan said, noticing Dot's reaction. He laughed. "While Abigail loves attention."

Indeed, Abigail was rubbing her face against Savannah's arm, eager for more.

Savannah laughed too, delighted by the huge, gentle creatures. Maisie was last, alone in her stall. When Savannah approached, she noticed that the pregnant cow was pacing and pawing around. "Something's going on with Maisie."

Logan hurried down the barn aisle and studied the cow. "Yep, she's getting ready."

"You mean she's going to give birth? How long will that take?" Savannah was excited to see a brand-new baby cow. They were so cute, with their long, wobbly legs.

Logan shrugged. "Depends on the cow." He checked Maisie's hay and water to make sure they were full, then said, "Let's leave her alone."

"I hope she gives birth while I'm here." Savannah glanced back at the cow. "Good luck, Maisie."

An hour later, Savannah was almost finished cleaning the stalls when she heard a low moo. Was that Maisie? It had to be, since she and the cow were the only ones left in the barn. The other cows were grazing in the fields.

She put aside the scraper and trotted out of the stall area and down to Maisie's pen. The cow was lying on the floor. Was it happening right now? Savannah ran from the barn, searching for Roy and Logan. She saw them down by the farm stand, opening the service window.

"Maisie is having her baby cow!" A second later, she realized the correct term was *calving*. Oh well, she was excited.

The two men conferred, and then Logan trotted her way while Roy stayed at the stand to serve an early customer.

When Logan reached Savannah, they hurried toward the barn while Savannah related Maisie's behavior.

"Sounds like things are moving right along," Logan said. "It shouldn't take very long once labor begins."

Inside the barn, Savannah watched while Logan assessed Maisie's condition and progress. "She's doing fine," he announced. "Now we stand back and let her do her thing."

Logan pulled up a couple of pails so they could sit outside the stall, near enough to help if necessary but not close enough to bother the laboring mother.

As they waited, he told stories about previous births he'd attended. "I might add cows or goats to my farm at some point. But they are a whole other level of work. I'm not quite ready for that."

After lending a hand in the barn and observing how Roy cared for his herd, Savannah fully appreciated the commitment involved. The cows were like four-legged family members. In fact, she was so excited and anxious about the impending birth that she was digging her nails into her palms.

"And here we go." Logan stood to lean on the railing. "We've got a new calf. Good job, Mama."

At his awed words, tears sprang to Savannah's eyes, and goose bumps prickled all over her body. She joined Logan at the fence as Maisie went to her baby and began to lick the calf clean. "That's so sweet. And the calf is adorable." The little creature had big eyes and ears and long, gangly legs.

"I think it's a heifer," Logan said. "We'll need to take a closer look to be sure."

A heifer was a female, which meant another milk producer joining the herd. She jumped up and down, clasping her hands. "Can I name her? Please?"

Logan appeared amused. "Roy and Gladys have naming rights, but we can pass along your suggestion. What is it?"

Savannah thought for a moment, considering various possibilities. "I know," she finally said. "Annabelle."

"Annabelle," Logan repeated, settling his cap more firmly on his head. "I like it."

Maisie nudged the calf to a standing position, and the young one took a few tentative, wide-legged steps.

Savannah burst into tears. "It's so wonderful."

"How's it going in here?" Roy appeared in the barn doorway, walking slowly with his crutch. "Did she deliver?"

"You just missed it," Savannah said. "Come see baby Annabelle. She's so cute."

"Annabelle, huh? I guess we can live with that." Roy winked at Savannah. "I'd better tell Gladys the news." The farmer took his phone out of his pocket and made the call. "You might want to come out here," he told his wife. "We have a new addition."

Gladys ran right out to the barn, and the foursome spent some time admiring the new arrival and making sure Maisie was all right. Then they adjourned to the house for a coffee break.

As Savannah trudged to the house, still dressed in awkward rubber boots and overalls, hair a mess and body aching with tiredness, she realized something. She was happy in a quiet, contented kind of way. Who would have guessed that she would actually enjoy working on a farm?

And as she watched Logan laugh at one of Roy's jokes, she admitted another startling fact. Being around Logan had a lot to do with her happiness.

After the break, Savannah worked the counter of the farm stand. Even now, at the tail end of the growing season, there was a steady stream of customers. Pumpkins, squash, and potatoes were popular.

The cooler held bunches of kale from Logan's farm, and she was glad to see those sell quickly too.

Local young mother Emily returned, along with her kids, Anya and Oliver.

Savannah braced herself, hoping that Emily wouldn't take any more pictures. She'd been afraid to search for the ones of her with the chickens.

Emily steered her children toward the pile of pumpkins. "Each of you can pick one out. Then we'll carve them into jack-o'-lanterns."

Anya and Oliver set to work examining the pumpkins.

"Hi again," Emily said, smiling at Savannah. "The kids have been talking all week about coming to see the chicken lady."

Savannah pasted a smile on her face and tried to take comfort in the fact that she was now one of the farm's attractions. "I'm glad you did," she said, then changed the subject. "We've got all kinds of interesting squash today." She held up a round squash known as red kuri. Another round type with a lump on top was called turban squash.

Emily regarded them dubiously. "What do they taste like? The kids don't really care for squash."

"To be honest, I haven't tried them. But I'm sure they're good, or Roy and Gladys wouldn't grow them." Savannah pointed to a rack of index cards on the counter. "Recipes are right there if you want to check them out."

Oliver screamed, protesting something his sister had done, so Emily dashed out to the pumpkins. Through the open window, Savannah heard her comforting Oliver while gently scolding Anya.

To keep busy, Savannah checked over the bins and consolidated some of the vegetables.

"How's it going?" Logan entered the stand, a bushel of potatoes on his hip.

"Perfect timing. We're low on those." Savannah stood aside so he could pour the tubers into the bin. "I love potatoes. Especially when mashed with lots of butter and cream."

Logan grinned. "There's a restaurant in town that makes a mean mashed potato." He cleared his throat. "In fact, I was going to—"

Savannah's phone gave a distinctive chime from under the counter, where she'd stashed it. "Hold that thought. I'm sorry, but I have to take this." She ran to answer before voice mail kicked in. "Hello?" she said, hoping she didn't sound too breathless.

"Is this Savannah Prescott?" a woman with an English accent asked.

"Yes, it is," Savannah said.

"Please hold for Fiona."

Savannah sagged against the counter, trying to calm down. Fiona Bates was the designer Savannah most wanted to work for. If she were chosen to represent her clothing, other designers would flock to hire her too.

"Hello, darling," a voice drawled. "Is this a good time?"

Savannah glanced over her shoulder. Logan was helping Emily and the kids with the pumpkins, and there weren't any other customers. But if there had been, she still would have taken the call. Fashion was her life. Working at the farm was only a temporary sidebar. But was Logan? She hastily cut off that train of thought. Now was not the time.

"Of course," she said, injecting a smile into her voice. "I'm thrilled to hear from you."

Fiona laughed and said, "We're glad that you reached out to us. We've been searching for new brand reps for a while. And you're perfect."

Was this really happening? Savannah pinched herself on the inner arm to make sure she was awake. "I'm glad you think so," she squeaked, barely suppressing a shout of pure joy. "Your designs are incredible. So gorgeous but wearable." She meant it. Some clothing looked good on a tiny model but terrible on real people. Fiona cut her clothing to flatter bodies of all shapes and sizes.

"That's what I'm aiming for," Fiona said. "What's the point if only a small percentage of the population can wear my clothes?" She paused. "You're trim but approachable. I already thought so. Then I saw those shots of you with the chickens. Totally adorable."

Savannah released a breath she didn't know she was holding. Instead of making her a laughingstock, Emily's snapshots seemed to have clinched the deal. She owed the young mother for that one.

"So when can I see you?" Fiona asked. By her brisk tone, Savannah sensed the designer was ready to conclude the call.

"Whenever is good for you," Savannah hastily said. "I can clear my calendar."

"Let me check something." The phone was muffled briefly, but Savannah could discern a couple of voices talking. Fiona came back. "How about tomorrow afternoon at four? My office." She rattled off the address.

Savannah hardly had time to agree before the designer disconnected.

Stunned, Savannah stared at her phone. She couldn't believe she had an interview with Fiona.

The voices of Logan and Emily interrupted her reverie.

Savannah glanced up to see them approaching the farm stand with Anya and Oliver following.

Logan set two pumpkins on the counter. "You picked the best ones," he told the kids with a grin.

After Emily paid for the pumpkins, the trio said goodbye and headed for their car.

Once Savannah and Logan were alone, he turned to her. "As I was saying earlier, there's a great restaurant in town. I was wondering if you'd like to go out to dinner with me tonight?"

Savannah knew she should tell Logan about her interview in New York. But she didn't have the nerve to break the news. Besides, it was only dinner, right?

She smiled and said, "I'd love to."

Amy

After leaving the arts center, Amy went downtown searching for lunch. Why Thai looked good, so she stepped inside. The restaurant was filling up quickly, but Amy was able to snag a small table.

As she was perusing the menu, a woman with red hair and dramatic eye makeup approached. After a moment, Amy recognized Missy Perkins, the director of the chamber of commerce.

"I thought that was you," Missy said with a wide smile. "Are you enjoying your time in Magnolia Harbor?"

"I am." Amy folded her menu, having decided on the vegetable stir-fry with tofu, one of her favorite Thai dishes. "I spent the morning at the arts center making coffee mugs."

"That sounds fun." Missy glanced at the counter, where people were lined up for takeout meals. "I was hoping to dash in and get an order to go."

On impulse, Amy asked, "Why don't you sit with me? If you have the time."

"Thank you." Missy slid into the seat across from Amy. "It's not that I have to return to my office right away, but I usually work through lunch." She sighed. "It's nice to actually take a break."

Amy felt a pang of recognition at Missy's comment. She worked through lunch and even dinner all the time. At least her company had an on-site cafeteria with great food. But still . . .

"You seem lost in thought," Missy remarked as she picked up a menu. "Are you wondering about what to eat?"

"No, I've already decided," Amy said. "I was thinking about my job and how I never go out to lunch unless it's a work meeting."

Before Missy could respond, a server approached the table. "Good afternoon," the woman said with a smile. "Welcome to Why Thai. What can I get you?"

After Amy and Missy ordered, the server deposited two glasses of ice water and buzzed off with a promise to bring the food quickly.

"The food and the service are great here." Missy took the paper off a straw and dunked it into the water. "So what do you do?"

Amy told Missy about her job. She mentioned that Abel worked in the same field but in a different company. "We're just a couple of hardworking nerds," she concluded.

"I'll bet," Missy said. "But it sounds like you love your job, so it's all good, right?"

Amy laughed in response. No, she didn't love her job. Yes, she was hooked on the pace, the challenges, the adrenaline rush of hitting goals and beating out competitors, but she wasn't passionate about the actual work.

Missy sent her a questioning look.

"Sorry," Amy said. "I wasn't laughing at you or what you said. If you'd asked me a week ago, I would have said that I love my job." She folded her arms on the table and leaned forward. "But after staying here in Magnolia Harbor, I'm getting a whole new perspective."

Missy brushed her angled bangs back and fluttered her thick black lashes. "I guess that's good news?" Her voice rose in inquiry.

Amy laughed again. "I think it is. I'm completely rethinking my career path." She leaned back as the server placed two steaming bowls of fragrant stir-fried vegetables on the table.

Missy picked up her ceramic spoon. "Really? Tell me more."

"I have a feeling my grandmother would like my idea." Amy smiled. "And you're the ideal person to run it by."

An hour later, full of delicious food and helpful advice, Amy strolled down to the park. Missy had been very receptive to her fledgling idea, and she had even tossed in a few suggestions. All in all, Amy was encouraged that she was on the right track.

The only stumbling block was getting her husband on board. But surely Abel would see the utter perfection of the idea.

As she ambled along, studying the historic, charming buildings and saying hello to friendly passersby, she felt totally at home. As if she belonged here.

Amy never felt that way in Atlanta. At least, not entirely. There her worth was based on her latest triumphs, the size of her bank account, the status of her address, and the make and model of her car. Those were the rules of that particular game, and until now, she'd been happy to play. To be completely honest, winning was her aim.

Maybe her drive had been misdirected. She was a descendant of Jeremiah Prescott, who had been followed by a long line of businessmen—and women, including her grandmother.

Her musings occupied her all the way to the waterfront. There she decided to work her way through the booths one by one. She'd already seen the pottery and enjoyed it a great deal. But now she had another aim.

The first booth, run by Smith Pottery, featured a display of beautiful plates and pots with etched floral and leaf designs. The work reminded Amy of classical pottery but with an updated flair.

After studying the pieces, she approached the potter, a tall man with a runner's build and cropped gray hair. "Is this your work? I love it."

"It is," he said. "I'm Tim Smith. This is my twentieth year in business." He pointed to a display board. "I use a wood-fired kiln I built on family property."

They chatted about his process and his work for a few minutes. He explained how he sold directly from his shop, through several galleries, and select shows like this one.

"I'd love more sales." Tim shrugged. "But I've bumped up against the limits of what I can do to make that happen."

Amy took a deep breath. This was the opening she had been waiting for. "I've been thinking . . ."

The rest of the afternoon went like that, with most people responsive to her idea. She arrived back at the inn with a ton of business cards and a few purchases.

Winnie was working behind the desk. "Good afternoon. Did you have a good day?"

Amy set her items down on the counter. "I sure did." She pointed to a blue-and-silver vase. "I'd like to give this to the inn as a gift."

Winnie's eyes widened. "It's gorgeous. Grace will love using it with her garden flowers." She bustled around the corner of the desk. "Let's put it in a safe place."

"By the way, I used the tool you gave me," Amy said as she trailed the older woman to the dining room.

"I'm glad." Winnie placed the vase on a side table, where it looked pretty even without flowers.

"It's used to decorate pottery," Amy added.

"Is that so?" Winnie said. "By the way, you and Abel will be the only two eating here tonight. Savannah and Dylan will be out, and I think Phillip has dinner plans too."

"That's okay," Amy said. She pictured eating by candlelight, just the two of them. When was the last time that had happened? She couldn't even remember. "Have you seen my husband?"

Winnie glanced toward the lake. "He was taking a kayak out. But that was a while ago, so he should be back soon."

Amy went to the window and peered at the lake. She only saw a fishing boat puttering past. The afternoon sun was starting to set, which meant the temperature would be dropping. She hoped he wouldn't get too chilled.

Speaking of which, a long, hot bath sounded good right now. She gathered her belongings and headed up to the Dogwood Suite.

After rummaging through her clothing and choosing a silky tunic with leggings to wear, she ran the bathwater, pouring in deliciously scented bubble bath provided by the inn.

As Amy moved about the suite, she was startled to find herself humming. She paused in the middle of the room, a pair of stockings in her hand. The ever-present cloud of expectation and pressure that weighted her every waking moment was gone. She had nothing on her mind except relaxing with a magazine in the bath. And maybe putting on fresh nail polish afterward.

She floated toward the bathroom to turn off the water, thinking that she could certainly get used to this. Goodbye, corporate job. Goodbye, city lifestyle.

Amy was curled up in a chair reading a book when Abel returned, ruddy and cold from his time on the lake. "Don't you look nice?" he said, his eyes lighting up.

"Thank you." Amy inclined her head. A knot lodged in her belly. Tonight over dinner, she was going to share her plan with Abel. She was a tiny bit afraid of how he would respond. "Why don't you get warmed up with a shower? We're the only two having dinner tonight."

"Good. I mean, I love your family, but it'll be nice to have the evening to ourselves." Abel grabbed some clothing from his suitcase and went to the bathroom. A moment later, the water turned on, and she heard him singing.

Amy returned to her book, but she was too distracted to read. Instead, she kept replaying the conversations she'd had today. A familiar pulse of excitement accompanied her thoughts, but for the first time, it was around her own project, not one that belonged to her company.

She savored her elation and anticipation for a moment. Of course, she might well fail, but she hadn't felt so alive in ages. And somehow she sensed that Grammie would approve. She'd always pushed Amy, Dylan, and Savannah to think for themselves and be leaders, not followers. And Amy had been a leader to a point. But company hierarchy limited her ability to change anything. Higher-ups hadn't always appreciated her input. Now she could make the decisions. What a heady idea.

"You look lost in thought." Abel checked his appearance in front of the full-length mirror. He wore a green button-down she liked with a pair of dress slacks.

Amy laughed, not wanting to disclose her idea yet. "Yes, just sitting here daydreaming." She put a bookmark between the pages of her book. "Ready to go downstairs?"

"Let's go." Abel led the way to the dining room.

Charlotte had set a small table near the windows. China and silver gleamed in soft, flickering candlelight, and in the middle of the table sat Amy's vase, filled with red and white roses.

"This is spectacular," Amy said as Abel held out her chair. She cupped a rose blossom, releasing its sweet fragrance.

"Those are from our garden," Charlotte said, entering the room. "The last of the roses." She waited for Abel to sit, then said, "I've got roasted butternut squash soup to start, followed by miso-glazed eggplant bowls with basil. All local produce."

"Sounds amazing," Amy said, unfolding her napkin and placing it on her lap.

Charlotte brought them glasses of white wine, then disappeared into the kitchen. Soft classical music played on hidden speakers, and across the room, the gas log fireplace provided a warm glow.

Amy wanted to ask Abel about his interview, but instead she said, "Tell me about your paddle today."

Abel described how he'd circled one of the islands, which ended up being more work than he'd counted on. "But once I was halfway around, it was equal work either way, so I kept going." He pressed on a bicep with a grin. "At least I got a good workout."

"So did I, walking around town for hours." She veered away from dangerous territory, not ready to spill the beans yet. "I had a delicious lunch at a little place called Why Thai."

"That's nice. I—" Abel broke off as Charlotte appeared with two bowls. Toasted croutons and sunflower seeds floated on top of the creamy soup.

"Would you like another glass of wine?" the chef asked.

Amy realized her glass was empty. She was drinking too fast due to nerves. "No, thank you. But I will take water, please."

Abel also wanted water, and Charlotte went to a sideboard to pour two tall glasses from a pitcher.

"If I'd seen that, I could have gotten us glasses," Amy said.

"No problem." Charlotte set tinkling glasses in front of them. "Your dinner will be out soon." She left the room again.

"Before you tell me about your interview, there is something I want to say." Amy forced her suddenly stiff lips to smile. "Something important." She couldn't hold back a moment longer.

He cocked his head, a quizzical expression in his eyes. "Okay, go ahead."

Amy picked up her spoon and swirled the soup, then took a taste. It was excellent. "As you know, I went to the pottery studio this morning. I made us mugs."

Abel scooped up soup. "Can't wait to see them." By the flatness of his tone, he knew she was stalling.

"Anyway," Amy said, keeping her gaze on her bowl, "I had a great idea. And I talked to some people today who agreed with me. About a dozen potters or so."

"You're going to support the festival?" Abel asked. "Follow in your grandmother's footsteps?"

Amy took a deep breath. "Sort of. Well, a little more than that." She swallowed. "I want to start a company that markets local pottery to high-end stores and online."

"Sounds like a cool idea," he said. Then he narrowed his eyes. "You mean part-time or full-time?"

"I was thinking full-time." Amy traced a design on the damask tablecloth with her finger. "A fair amount of travel will be involved." She'd have to visit large vendors and go to trade shows and visit the pottery studios. "Besides, if I'm going to do it, I want to do it well."

Abel continued to stare at her, his jaw working. "Are you sure about ditching your career? If you decide to go back, it won't be at your current level. You know how fast tech moves."

Amy had thought about that. She compared it to climbing a slippery mountain. Once she allowed herself to slide backward, she'd never regain the same ground.

"I understand that, and I know it's a risk." She felt tears burn in her eyes. "But it makes me feel passionate. And alive. I had such a wonderful time today talking with the potters. Their work is incredible. But they need someone to market it for them."

"Hmm." Abel took a spoonful of soup and ate it. "I guess I don't have any objections. It's not my place to have any. But you'll need to do it from California. I really want that job."

Amy's heart sank. She fully understood his point of view. But she'd realized that she needed to do this work from the South, preferably in South Carolina, close to her producers. Plus, she wanted the lifestyle. Living in beautiful but urban California felt like the wrong direction.

"What is it?" he said, his tone sharp. He tossed his napkin onto the table. "Come on. Spill it."

Now the tears overflowed. "I don't want to move to California. I'm sorry, but I just don't. I want to stay in the South. And not in Atlanta either." Every fiber of her being craved the sweet peace she'd discovered in small-town life. She was tired of the city.

Abel pushed back his chair and stood. "I guess we have to agree to disagree then, because I want to move. I had a fantastic interview by the way. Thank you for asking."

"Where are you going?" A stab of panic lanced through Amy. She loved Abel, and she had every intention of honoring her marriage commitment. But had she honestly thought he would change his goals and direction because she expressed her deepest desires? No, the pattern was that Abel set the pace, and Amy went along for the ride. He'd had the final word on every decision throughout their entire marriage.

He shoved his chair under the table. "I'm going out for a while. I need to think."

For a split second, the old insecurity reared up, pouring ice water through Amy's veins. The panic became a shrilling alarm in her ears. The old Amy would have folded, would have retracted her words to placate him.

But then her spine stiffened. "Go ahead. But I'm serious about this. We only get one life, and as much as I love you, the one we're leading isn't the one I want anymore." She rose. "If that means to you that I've broken our deal, then I'm sorry."

"Deal?" His face twisted. "What deal? I never . . ." With a growl, he stormed out the door.

Amy collapsed into her chair. The front door slammed, and a moment later, she heard the roar of an engine.

Then the tears came fast and furious.

21

Grace

The entrance doors at Northshore Medical Center swished open, a sound that brought back a host of painful memories to Grace. Years ago, her mother had died in this hospital from complications of pneumonia, and now she was visiting a young man with the same ailment. Evan had been admitted earlier that day upon the advice of his doctors. With his multiple health conditions, they wanted to be extra cautious.

Grace rested the bouquet of flowers she held against the front desk. Of course, young Evan wouldn't care less about flowers, but Grace thought his mother and grandmother would appreciate the gesture. And the well-wishes on the card tucked inside.

"Can you direct me to Evan Halstead's room?" Grace asked the attendant.

While the woman was searching for the information, the doors opened.

Spencer strode through the doorway, his brow furrowed, and walked over to Grace. "I take it you're here to see Evan?"

"Yes, I am," Grace said. "And to provide moral support. His poor family. As if they haven't been through enough as it is."

"Any word on how he's doing?" he asked.

Grace shook her head. Through the glass, she spotted another familiar figure approaching. "Dylan's here." Her heart lifted. Somehow she hadn't imagined the self-involved young man would bother to visit.

"Any news?" Dylan asked. Worry creased his handsome features.

"Not yet," Grace said. "We're heading up once we get the room number."

"He's in 212," the attendant said. "He has limited visitation, but there's a waiting room on that floor."

The trio walked in silence toward the elevators, their shoes squeaking on the freshly waxed tiles. Spencer pushed the up button, and after a short delay, the elevator arrived. The two men stood back to let Grace enter first.

The waiting room was right off the bank of elevators, marked with a sign over the door. Grace spotted Mia, pacing back and forth across the small space. Etta was crocheting.

Grace set the flowers down and gave the teen and her grandmother a hug of greeting. "How is he?"

Spencer and Dylan crowded into the room behind her, both waiting anxiously for the answer.

"They've got him on an antibiotic IV," Etta said. "Kelli's in there right now. Hopefully she'll have more answers when she gets back."

"I sure hope he'll be better soon." Dylan's throat worked with emotion. "He's a great kid." He quickly wiped his eyes with the back of his hand.

Etta paused her handwork, compassion in her eyes. "Evan thinks highly of you too. Lately, all he's been talking about is being an architect when he grows up."

Mia plopped down on a chair, resting her stocking feet on the seat. "Yeah. He told me he wants to build happy homes for families."

Evan was such a sweet and special young man. Feeling her eyes well up, Grace fumbled in her jacket pocket for a tissue and blew her nose. "Can we get you anything to eat or drink from the cafeteria?" She guessed that the family hadn't taken time for dinner, and it was almost seven o'clock.

"I'm not that hungry, but we should eat something," Etta said, then turned to her granddaughter. "How about we share a sandwich?"

After a brief discussion, they told Grace they wanted a turkey club sandwich and a container of soup for Kelli.

"She's got to eat," Etta said. "Soup should settle okay."

"I'll go with you," Spencer said to Grace. "I could use a cup of coffee."

Dylan reached into his pocket and pulled out his wallet. "It's on me. And I'll have a coffee too. Thanks."

"No, it's on me," Spencer insisted when Dylan tried to hand him a few bills. "We'll be right back."

Grace and Spencer took the elevator downstairs again.

"I feel so helpless," Grace remarked as they walked toward the cafeteria.

"I know," Spencer said, following her toward the food counter. "All we can do is pray."

At this time of night, no one else was in the cafeteria, and only one person—a tall African American man wearing a long apron—was working behind the line.

"What can I get you?" he asked. "We've got hot turkey dinners, or I can make you fresh sandwiches. All the packaged ones are gone."

"I prefer fresh anyway," Grace said with a smile. She placed the order for a turkey club, then asked about soup.

"We have some chicken noodle left," the cook said.

"We'll take a bowl," Grace said.

"Want coffee while we wait for the food?" Spencer asked Grace.

She agreed, and they dispensed cups of the brew, then sat down at a table.

To their surprise, Dylan and Tabitha walked in. Seeing Spencer and Grace, they diverted over to the table.

"Tabitha wanted dinner, so I thought I'd come down for coffee." Dylan's eyes pleaded for them not to reveal he'd already asked them to get him a cup.

Spencer pushed out a chair. "Have a seat. We're drinking coffee while we wait for food to take up to the Halsteads."

Tabitha ordered while Dylan fetched two cups of coffee. After Dylan paid for the food and drinks, the pair sat down.

"I was visiting clients out of town, and I came straight here." Tabitha stirred her coffee with a little red stick. "I was so shocked to hear the news."

"Me too," Grace said. "Winnie and I were at House to Home, and we saw Kelli rush out of Hanson's next door. That must have been when Evan got sick."

"I was hoping they'd give Evan medicine and let him go home," Tabitha said. "But they decided to admit him."

Dylan stared down into his cup as if it held all the answers. "The last few days have turned me upside down." He leaned back and gestured at the quiet room. "If you told me a week ago that I'd be sitting here, worried sick about someone I just met, let alone a kid, I would have laughed you out of the room. I was too busy with my big job and my fancy friends to care about anything else." His tone was bitter with regret and self-reproach.

Tabitha watched Dylan closely, tenderness in her eyes again, but she didn't say anything.

"The same sort of thing happened to me," Spencer said unexpectedly. "I was an intelligence analyst for the FBI in Fredericksburg. My career was all-consuming, even more so after the death of my wife. But moving to Magnolia Harbor was exactly what I needed." He inhaled deeply, then released a sigh. "A simple life but a meaningful one."

"Well put," Grace said. Spencer didn't talk much about his past, and she never probed. She'd also experienced grief when she lost her husband two decades ago. After growing up in Magnolia Harbor, she'd left town for college at Clemson and her job at a top marketing firm. But she'd returned home to a most beloved town full of wonderful people.

"Soup and sandwich to go," the cook called.

"That's our cue," Spencer said, standing.

Grace swallowed the last of her coffee and pushed back her chair. "See you upstairs."

"We'll be there soon," Tabitha said.

As Grace walked away, she heard the social worker ask Dylan, a hint of challenge in her tone, "Ever think about making a change?"

"Actually, now that you mention it," Dylan replied, "I have."

Grace hurried to the counter, not wanting to eavesdrop. But secretly she was thrilled. Dorothy Prescott's unorthodox plan was bearing fruit, at least with her grandson.

The cook gave them the soup and sandwich, and Grace decided to pick up bottled water, chips, potato salad, and some dessert too.

Spencer insisted on paying for the food and drinks. Then they took their purchases and walked down the corridor.

"I'm impressed with the changes in Dylan," Spencer said once they reached the privacy of the elevator. "He's like a different person."

"Maybe he's becoming who he was meant to be," Grace said. "The rest of it was all trappings and ego to fit in with the people around him."

Spencer nodded. "Very astute. I think you're right." When the elevator opened on the second floor, he took a step back to let her exit first, his arm guarding the door from sliding closed too soon.

Etta and Mia glanced up when they entered the waiting room. The older woman was still crocheting, and Mia was occupied with her phone. The teen set the phone aside, her gaze fixed on the food. "I guess I am kind of hungry," she said.

"Good," Grace said. She set the food and drinks on a table. "I grabbed some double chocolate brownies too. I hope you like those."

Mia's squeal of joy was gratifying. Brownies had a way of making things a little bit better.

Mia took a seat at the table, followed by Etta, and the two dug into the light meal.

"Kelli's in with the doctor now," Etta said, forestalling their questions. "She'll have an update for us when she comes out." One hand went to the cross she wore around her neck, and she held it as though seeking comfort and hope.

Spencer and Grace took adjacent seats.

"How did it go at the construction site today?" Grace asked. After she'd left, the teams had continued on. She assumed they'd worked until dark.

"Everything went really well," Spencer replied. "The windows and doors are in so we're starting the drywall tomorrow. And a crew is putting up the siding. Pretty soon we'll be ready for paint and flooring."

"We ordered that today," Grace said. She retrieved the sample cards from her handbag and passed them over, explaining what was going where. She couldn't focus on what she was saying, and she thought the same was true of Spencer. They were trying to distract themselves. Meanwhile, a knot sat in her stomach, growing as the minutes ticked by.

"Hey," a soft voice said from the doorway. Kelli stood there, along with a man dressed in a doctor's coat. A huge smile broke across Kelli's face. "We've got great news. Evan is over the hump. He's going to be okay."

22

Savannah

As Savannah got ready for her dinner date with Logan, she replayed the phone call from Fiona for about the tenth time. She hadn't been able to think about anything else. Tomorrow her new life would begin.

With a shiver, Savannah slid her feet into a pair of platform heels. They were perfect with her black dress. She moved to the full-length mirror to check her appearance, twirling around for good measure.

She hoped Logan would approve of her outfit. At the thought of the farmer, anticipation and trepidation warred in equal measure. She was looking forward to seeing him tonight, no question. But she'd have to divulge her news about New York, since she had been too much of a coward to do so at the farm.

Why didn't she tell him? Savannah couldn't help but think of her grandmother. Grammie had been a stickler for honesty, and she'd rooted out half-truths, fibs, and little white lies like a bloodhound. Savannah and her siblings often said Grammie was like a judge, expecting the truth, the whole truth, and nothing but the truth.

Savannah hadn't told Logan because she knew he wasn't going to be happy about her taking off for New York. Her time at the farm wasn't over, and besides that, he was starting to care. She could tell. But she couldn't turn Fiona down. This was her big break, and hopefully he'd see it that way. If not . . . Savannah lifted her chin. She'd have to be a big girl and deal with his reaction.

Sometimes in life you couldn't have it all. This was probably one of those times.

Savannah's phone went off. Logan had sent a text, saying he was here. She glanced in the mirror one last time, then grabbed her handbag and a coat.

Logan's eyes widened when Savannah came down the stairs.

So did hers when she saw him. Until now, she'd only seen him dressed casually. While handsome in jeans and a flannel shirt, he looked amazing in dress pants and a dark-green shirt. He wore a sleek black leather jacket and boots with the ensemble, and his hair was neatly styled.

"You clean up nice," Savannah teased.

Logan gave her a cocky grin. "I could say the same for you, though there haven't been any mishaps lately."

She laughed.

Logan helped her put on her coat, then leaned close. "You look lovely tonight," he whispered.

The sincerity in his voice made her heart leap. "Thank you, kind sir." She turned around and slid her handbag strap over her shoulder. "Where are you taking me?"

"One of my favorite places. Turner's Lakeside Grill." He opened the door for her, guiding her out with a hand on her lower back.

Logan had brought his truck. Savannah could tell it had been freshly washed, maybe even waxed. Inside, it was pristine. The scent of pine drifted from the air freshener.

With a smile, he started the engine and backed out of the parking space, his attention on the task of conveying her safely to their destination. That was the feeling she got anyway, and with every sweet gesture, she felt a little bit smaller.

Savannah didn't deserve him. Or rather, he deserved someone who wanted to share his life. Someone who liked getting up at dawn and working until dusk. Someone who enjoyed fresh air and the smell of animal barns too. This last thought startled a laugh from her.

Logan glanced over. "What's so funny?"

"Nothing," Savannah said. "Just one of those crazy random thoughts."

Seeming to accept her answer, he returned his gaze to the road. "What a nice night. Look at that. People have jack-o'-lanterns out. I wonder if they bought those pumpkins from us."

Thinking of Emily and her children, Savannah said, "Maybe they did." It was fun seeing the seasonal decorations in front of Magnolia Harbor's pretty houses.

As they continued driving, Savannah remembered Winnie telling her that Phillip was taking Julep to The Tidewater for dinner tonight. Savannah hoped the nice older man was having a good time. Babysitting them must be a chore for him, although she supposed there were worse client requests than staying in Magnolia Harbor.

"As promised," Logan said, signaling and turning into a parking lot. "Turner's Lakeside Grill, located—you guessed it—on the lake." He slid into a spot. "Stay put. I'm coming around."

Feeling delightfully cherished, she waited for him.

He opened the door and helped her out, which was quite a step down from the high truck cab, and she stumbled. "You okay?" He steadied her with his arm until she nodded.

They strolled arm in arm toward the restaurant.

Partway there, Logan stopped. "Would you look at that moon?" His voice was as proud as if he'd ordered it up just for her.

Savannah drank in the sight of the full moon rising over the lake, a trail of silver left in its wake. She pulled out her phone. "I've got to get a picture of it."

Logan chuckled. "I've never seen anyone take so many photos."

She leaned close to show him the shot. "I like to record the moments." She scrolled back to an earlier picture of Maisie and her calf, Annabelle. The cows had their heads close together in an adorable display of love. "Check out this photo."

"Nice," Logan said. "Send it to me, and I'll post it for Roy on his farm's social media page." He made a face. "Yeah, you're right. I should get one too."

Hiding a smile over his admission, Savannah sent the photo to him, along with a couple more. He opened the door for her, and she smiled as she stepped past him into the restaurant.

A hostess station stood right in front of them, with the restaurant extending beyond. At this time of night, the restaurant was fairly full.

"Good evening," the hostess said. "Two for dinner?"

Logan nodded.

With a practiced move, the hostess grabbed two tall menus out of the holder. "Follow me."

The hostess led the way to a corner table by the windows. Although all Savannah could see was the restaurant reflected in the windows, it felt cozy and private over here.

"Your server will be right with you," the hostess said, placing the menus on the table.

"The food is great." Logan picked up his menu. "Everything is homemade."

Glancing over the meat and seafood choices, Savannah was glad she wasn't a vegan, like her sister. The four-ounce steak was perfect for her appetite. She closed the menu. "I'm thinking the small rib eye, medium-rare, with a baked potato and salad."

Logan raised one brow. "That was fast." He closed his menu. "I'll have the same, only the eight-ounce steak."

"Not attempting the twenty-ounce rib eye tonight?" Savannah teased.

He made a growling grunt like a caveman and pounded his chest, then laughed. "I'm on a diet."

"Yeah, right." Savannah rolled her eyes. "My brother would order it. He's on a high-protein diet." She shuddered. "Hardly any carbs."

Logan grabbed a roll out of the basket. "That will never be me. Bring on the bread and potatoes." In the middle of buttering his roll, he glanced up. "I'm sorry. You can't eat these, can you?"

Touched that he remembered her gluten intolerance, she shook her head. "Please go ahead. I'm used to being deprived." She made a mock sobbing sound.

A young woman in a green apron arrived at the table. She pulled a notepad and a pen out of her pocket. "Hi, I'm Jen, and I'll be your server."

Logan waved the roll. "Do you have any gluten-free bread? My g—friend can't have gluten."

A thrill of shock ran down Savannah's spine. Had he almost said *girlfriend*? Not that she minded exactly, but it was much too soon. And besides, she was leaving town.

"No, I'm sorry. But we're working on it." Jen glanced at Savannah. "Next time." Swiveling her gaze between the pair, she asked, "What can I get you to drink?"

They selected iced tea and went ahead and ordered dinner too. Jen promised to bring their drinks and salads right away, then left.

Logan's face burned deep red. "Sorry about that." He ran a finger around the inside of his collar, as if it were too tight.

Savannah changed the subject to let him off the hook. "How are Maisie and Annabelle doing?" She was pleased that Roy had agreed to use the name she'd suggested.

He seized the topic with obvious relief. "They're doing well. When I checked in with Roy a little while ago, he said that Annabelle is eating."

Savannah couldn't hold back a smile at the thought of mother and baby. She'd never forget witnessing Annabelle's birth. "You'll have to keep me posted on her progress." *Oops.* She hadn't meant to say that. Not yet.

Before Logan could respond, Jen returned with a tray. She set down glasses of iced tea and bowls of salad. "Peppercorn poppy seed, oil, and vinegar."

After Jen walked away, they focused on pouring dressing on the salads and taking the first few bites.

Logan and Savannah started talking at the same time.

"You go first," he said.

"No, you." Savannah knew she was a wimp, but she hoped to buy a little time to organize her thoughts. What made it worse was that the evening was perfect so far. If only—*no.* She squared her shoulders. The door to her dream was open, and she had to step through it.

Logan took a deep breath and released it. "Savannah." The way he fiddled with his fork betrayed his nerves. He glanced down, then up, the intensity of his gaze causing her heart to skip a beat. "We haven't known each other long, and I know your life is in Atlanta. But I was hoping..." Another inhale. "I'd like to stay in touch. See where this is going."

Savannah's heart sank. No doubt about it, she was going to stomp on Logan's heart. How could a relationship with a South Carolina farmer, wonderful as he was, fit into her career as a top fashion influencer? Because that was one area she had no doubts about. Working for Fiona was only the beginning for her professional aspirations.

She'd better let him down as quickly and kindly as possible. "I've really enjoyed getting to know you." She winced at how lame that sounded.

"But?" Logan's brow furrowed as hurt flashed in his eyes. "I get it. This was all one-sided. You don't feel the same way."

"No, that's not true." Savannah's squirming became almost a dance. "I really, really like you. But I have to leave."

His frown deepened.

"I promise it has nothing to do with you. I got a job interview." She gulped. "In New York City." Another swallow. "I'm flying there tomorrow morning."

He slouched in his seat. "Okay, we can work with that."

"Logan," she said in a soft voice, "I'm sorry, but I don't think we can."

"So this is it?" With an incredulous laugh, Logan ran a hand over his hair. "When were you going to tell me?"

Savannah straightened her spine as if she'd been prodded. "I tried to tell you a few minutes ago. And besides, I thought we were just friends. I had no idea . . ." Grammie's voice rang in her mind, scolding her for the fib. But rather than admit her own hopes about them, she swallowed the words. What was the point now anyway? "If you want to cancel dinner, I'll understand."

Logan tilted his head and regarded her for a long moment. "Nope."

She gave him a questioning look.

"We're friends, like you said." He picked up his fork. "So let's enjoy our meal. And I want to hear all about your interview."

23

Amy

Amy was still wiping away tears when she heard footsteps. *Oh no.* She didn't want to see or talk to anyone right now. She rose from her chair, ready to flee. Then she glanced at the table, remembering they were in the middle of a meal. It wouldn't be right to disappear without saying anything to Charlotte.

But instead of Charlotte, Winnie walked in. For some reason, the sight of the kind older woman made the tears come again. Amy's chin even wobbled in a way it hadn't since childhood.

Winnie rushed over and gave her a big hug. "There, there," she murmured. "It will be all right."

"Nothing will ever be right again." Amy squeezed her eyes shut. First Grammie and now Abel. Would the losses ever end? And oh, the irony of thinking she had finally found her calling. Who could have guessed her husband would walk out in response?

She was barely aware of Winnie guiding her into the living room, where she settled her on a sofa. Amy didn't resist. Simply having the other woman near was comforting.

"Don't worry about dinner. I'll put away the food." Winnie patted Amy on the shoulder. "And I'll bring us a nice cup of tea." Without waiting for an answer, she exited the room to collect the dishes.

Amy collapsed against the sofa back and reached for a tissue from the convenient box on the side table. Every detail in this place was perfect. She swiped at her eyes and blew her nose, then reached for a second tissue. She hadn't cried like that in years, and she actually felt kind of good, as if she'd purged all her pain, doubts, and fears.

Including the tangle of unresolved grief and confusion from losing her parents. She hadn't even shared her discovery with Abel. Not that they usually discussed emotional issues or their personal histories. Maybe that was part of the problem.

The rattling of dishes preceded Winnie into the room. She carried a laden tray to the table in front of the sofa and gently set it down. "English tea, hot and fresh." She pointed to a plate of assorted cookies. "And vegan cookies. Help yourself."

Amy chose a cookie that looked like lemon and bit into it. She hummed in approval. "Did Charlotte make these?"

"She did." Winnie smoothed the back of her skirt and sat beside Amy, then poured two steaming cups of tea. "Almond milk is in the blue pitcher." After she slid the cup over to Amy, she added regular milk to her own.

There was a sugar bowl on the tray, and Amy dropped a spoonful into her cup, though she didn't usually use sugar. Wasn't sugared tea supposed to be good for an upset?

Winnie didn't say anything, but the silence was restful somehow. Finally, Amy said, "Thanks for this. I'm a mess at the moment."

"It happens." Winnie sipped her tea. "One of my grandmother's old sayings was that you can't make an omelet without breaking eggs." Another sip. "Sometimes things have to fall apart before they're put back together better than ever."

Amy grasped this idea like a lifeline. "You think so?" She felt the tears burn again but gulped them back. "I don't mind telling you that the last few days have upended my life." She laughed. "I thought I was happy—we were happy—but now I've called everything into question."

Winnie made a murmuring sound of acknowledgment. She set her cup down and lifted the pot. "Warm-up?"

"Thanks." Amy held out her cup. "But at least I think I know why Grammie wanted me to come to Magnolia Harbor." Behind the dark cloud of misery over Abel, Amy's new idea lit her mind and heart.

"And why is that?" Winnie asked, splashing a little more milk into her cup.

Amy shared her idea of promoting and selling handmade pottery from the region. "I really want to do this. It's creative and exciting, and it's going to benefit a lot of people. It feels right. Do you know what I mean?"

"I do," Winnie said. "I can see how fired up you are about it. And I agree that our local artisans deserve more attention. What does your husband think?"

Amy's head dropped. "That's just it. Abel's against the idea. Well, more against us staying in the South. He's seriously considering a job in California."

"I've often found that situations that seem impossible actually aren't." Winnie paused. "With a little compromise."

"In this case, I don't see how we can compromise." Amy bit her lip. "The opportunities require us to be on opposite coasts."

"Is that so?" Winnie stirred her tea, her motions as deliberate as her speech. "I understand that many people are telecommuting these days. A friend of mine has a son who lives in Atlanta, but he works for a company in London. His wife has a business that requires her to stay in the States."

A spark of hope lit in Amy's chest. She and Abel might be able to work things out so neither one of them had to sacrifice.

On impulse, Amy set down the tea and gave Winnie a hug. "Thank you, thank you, thank you. You helped me clarify things."

"No problem," Winnie said with a laugh. "That's what I'm here for."

After chatting for a while, Winnie stood. "My husband is going to wonder where I am. But before I go, I want to give you something." She returned a moment later with Amy's phone. "I thought you might need this."

Amy took the phone, the size and shape feeling strange in her hand. She'd gotten used to not carrying it around. But Winnie was right. She wanted to be reachable in case Abel called. But—

"Abel has his phone," Winnie said, as if reading her mind. "When I saw he was going for a drive, I thought he'd better take it." She picked up the tray. "Try to get some rest. I'll see you tomorrow." In the doorway, she halted. "There are some good novels in the music room."

"Thanks for the suggestion," Amy said. "I've got one in my room already."

"Have a nice evening." With a last, kind smile, Winnie was gone.

Amy got up and stretched, finding that her fears about the future of her marriage had ebbed for the moment. Curling up with a book on that plush, comfortable bed might help her relax even more.

Up in her suite, Amy changed into yoga pants and a T-shirt before climbing into bed with the book. She couldn't settle into reading, but using her phone held no attraction either. At one point, she checked to make sure she hadn't missed a call or a text from Abel. No such luck. But he probably didn't know she had her phone back.

So instead, she lay staring at the ceiling, hoping and praying that she and Abel would come to an understanding. But no matter what happened with him, the last few days had changed her in a deep and transformative way. For one thing, she was not going back to that toxic job. Just the thought of walking into her office made her pulse leap and her belly churn with stress.

She could see everything clearly now, as if she were an outsider observing Amy Butler's life. She realized that the constant connection demanded by her bosses had skewed her perspective to the point where being consumed by her job felt normal. So much so that she'd been lost at first without the scaffolding it provided for her thoughts and actions.

Did she dare quit? The thought made her dizzy, as if she were poised on the edge of a cliff. Then she gritted her teeth and snatched up her phone. Something had to give.

Once she unlocked it, the screen displayed her company's stock performance. It had skyrocketed over the last few days with the release of several new products.

As an employee, Amy received stock options as bonuses. Since she'd been there forever, most of them were vested, meaning she could cash out. Was it another sign she should leave? She decided to take it as one.

Despite the late hour, Amy placed a call to her immediate boss.

After the unpleasant task of resigning was done, Amy lay back against the pillows with a surge of relief. Her boss had been ticked off at first, but in the end, he'd left the door open in case she reconsidered. *No way*. She was never going back.

Footsteps sounded in the hall. Was Abel finally here? Amy slid off the bed and practically ran to the door. She cracked it open and peeked out.

Her spirits sank when she saw Savannah, heading across the hall toward her room. She must have made a noise because her sister glanced over. "Hey." Savannah's tone and the way her shoulders slumped told Amy something was wrong.

Welcome to the club. Amy stepped into the hall. "Want to talk about it?"

"I guess so. Can you come into my room? My feet are killing me." Savannah led the way inside, kicking off her shoes as she went.

"Love your outfit," Amy said. "You should help me pick out some new clothes." Now that she was launching an artsy new venture, she needed to switch up her look. No more corporate black. "I quit my job," she blurted out.

Savannah reared back, staring at Amy as if she'd sprouted another head. "Wait, what? You quit your job?" She dropped her handbag on the bureau, then slid out of her jacket, all without taking her gaze off her sister.

Amy plopped down on the side of the bed. "I sure did." Elation bubbled in her chest, making her giggle. "I feel great."

Her sister examined her closely, as if checking for illness or injury. "Well, good for you. What does Abel think?" She hung the jacket on a hanger and placed it in the closet.

There was the rub. "I haven't told him yet." Amy smoothed the bedspread, not meeting her sister's eyes. "We kind of had a fight earlier tonight." *Talk about an understatement.*

"You two?" Savannah said. "You never fight."

"Well, we do. Sort of. But this one was worse." Amy tried to swallow the lump in her throat. "I want to start a business here, but Abel wants to move to California." Her voice cracked, and tears started to flow again.

"Oh, hey." Savannah padded over to the bed. She grabbed a box of tissues and handed it to Amy, then sat beside her. She put a warm, comforting arm around Amy. "It's going to be okay. You guys love each other."

"You think? I mean, of course I love him. But we're both so busy we don't communicate that well." Amy blew her nose. "And now we've got this huge disconnect, and I don't know how we'll mend it."

"What's this business you want to start?" Savannah asked. She leaned her head against Amy's shoulder the way she used to when she was a little girl. But instead of baby powder, she now wore a sophisticated and most likely expensive perfume.

After Amy told her about the pottery business, Savannah said, "That sounds like something Grammie would want you to do."

"It does, doesn't it?" Amy sighed. "All I know is that the idea feels right in here." She tapped her chest. "So I can't ignore it."

Savannah gave a little whimper.

Amy pulled back slightly. "What's the matter?"

Savannah sat up and rubbed a hand across her face. She took a deep breath, then exhaled. "Fiona Bates wants to interview me."

Even Amy, buried in the tech world, knew who Fiona was. "That's fantastic! Congratulations." She hugged her sister. "When did this happen?"

Savannah told her about the call and the request to come to New York. She pushed herself off the bed and hurried to the closet. "I'd better pack now because I have to leave early tomorrow."

It sounded great, so why did Savannah seem upset? But before Amy could ask, she heard Abel calling her name in the hall, a familiar sound that made her heart start pounding. "I need to go." She gave Savannah a quick hug and a kiss on the cheek. "Safe travels. Keep me posted, okay?"

When she let herself out of the room, Abel was standing in the doorway of their suite, gazing around in puzzlement. His eyes flared when he spotted her, and relief flooded his face.

"I was in Savannah's room," she explained.

He crossed the hall in several long strides and gathered her into his arms. "I'm so sorry."

"Me too," she murmured, her voice muffled against his chest. "I'm glad you're back."

With his arm around her, Abel steered her into their suite. They sat on the edge of the bed, holding hands.

"I took a long ride. All the way to the coast." He paused. "We should go. The beach is gorgeous."

Amy pictured the ocean, the eternal breakers rolling in. "I'd like that." Now that he was here, she had no idea how to begin. She knew this discussion was critical to their marriage, and that made her afraid to blow it. Then it dawned on her. This was her pattern. Avoid conflict out of fear. If she and Abel loved each other, they could—and would—work it out.

"While you were gone, I did a lot of thinking," she said. "It might sound dramatic, but I need to start that business. It's the right thing for me to do. In fact, I quit my job tonight."

He gaped at her. "What are you talking—"

Amy put up a hand. "Let's shelve that until later. I know you want the job in California. So can we, two brilliant people who love each other, figure out a solution?" She gave him a quick kiss, then rested her forehead against his. "I bet we can."

24

Savannah

After Amy left, Savannah packed her bags. First she sorted out her newest and trendiest outfits designed by Fiona that she planned to wear in New York. She'd take a carry-on and leave the rest in her car in the airport parking lot.

While she was reorganizing her toiletries, her phone buzzed. It was a text from Logan. He told her to have a great trip, and he included a funny cartoon, which made her smile.

She quickly replied, adding a request to keep her updated on Annabelle. After watching the heifer's birth, she felt as proud as a parent. Well, maybe a godparent.

Logan promised to send pictures. He followed the message with a close-up photo of a cow's nose.

Laughing, Savannah set the phone on the bathroom counter, a wistful, homesick feeling sweeping over her. She already missed Logan. And Maisie and Annabelle, Roy and Gladys, even Emily and her rambunctious kids. But she'd get over it. She'd felt the same way when leaving summer camp and then college after graduation.

Savannah paused, a jar of skin cream in her hand. And how many fellow campers or college friends did she stay in touch with? She could count them on one hand. Most of her friends were getting married or having babies, and they were scattered across the country.

She shook her head. There was no point in getting sentimental. Sometimes paths diverged, and there was nothing that could be done about it. That was life, right?

Her sleep was fitful that night. She tossed and turned, unable to get comfortable despite her silk pajamas and the excellent mattress.

Savannah finally fell into a deep sleep right before her alarm went off. Groggy and grumpy, she jumped into the shower and then got dressed. She did full makeup and curled her hair, thinking ruefully of the days at the farm when she would simply wash her face and put her hair in a ponytail.

Carrying her bags, she gently shut the room door, not wanting to disturb the others. *Goodbye, Buttercup Suite.* She tiptoed downstairs to the foyer.

Phillip stood near the front desk, a cup of coffee in his hand. His unexpected appearance caused her to drop a suitcase, which thumped down the remaining steps. *So much for being quiet.*

Savannah put a hand over her racing heart. "You scared me." In the back of her mind, she'd been hoping she could escape without seeing him. But surely he wouldn't hold her to the unreasonable requirement of staying here any longer. She had to go to her interview today. She had no choice.

The attorney set his cup on the counter, then retrieved her bag and set it upright. "Sorry about that. I didn't mean to startle you." He rested his hands on his hips. "Going somewhere?"

Savannah smoothed her hair. "I'm headed to New York for an important job interview." She tried to smile, but her courage wilted under his intense stare. "This is the big break I've been waiting for."

Phillip crossed his arms. "You do realize that you are forfeiting your inheritance, according to the terms of your grandmother's will?"

In response, Savannah mirrored his gesture. "I suppose. Although I think the whole thing is ridiculous." Her thoughts flashed to her friends at the farm. They weren't ridiculous by any stretch. She'd never forget her time with them. She tossed her head again, making her earrings jingle. "Why would Grammie care if I spend so much time in Magnolia Harbor? Besides, I can always come back later."

"That's not an option. She wanted you all together." His eyes softened a trifle. "I'm not your enemy. I'm just carrying out my client's requests."

"Her requests are weird. I'm surprised we all didn't mutiny. But I guess we were too shocked about Grammie's death." Savannah extended the suitcase handle. "Excuse me, but I've got to get going."

Ever the gentleman, Phillip bent and grabbed the handles of her luggage, suppressing a grunt at the weight. "I'll help you take everything out to your car."

"Thanks. That's nice of you." Savannah gathered her belongings and led the way, her boot heels clicking across the foyer floor.

The attorney helped her load the car and wished her well, then went back inside the inn.

"Here we go," she whispered as she started the car, noticing that her palms were damp. Not wanting to rely on her memory, she pulled out her phone and checked the GPS map to the airport.

A notification of a new message popped onto her screen, with a picture of Logan and Roy in the milking parlor, smiling and waving. *The ladies miss you. So do we.*

Aww. How sweet. Savannah felt that wistful tug at her heart again. These guys were killing her.

Savannah drove out to the highway, making a brief stop for coffee to go. Then she got on the entrance ramp southbound and headed toward Charleston International Airport. It wasn't the most convenient thing to do, since she'd have to come back to South Carolina to get her car. Then if she landed the job, she would return to Atlanta and pack up her condo. Grammie had helped her buy it, and she didn't want to sell it. She hoped she wouldn't have much trouble finding a renter.

The highway was busy, and traffic grew heavier as rush hour began and she got closer to the city. Traffic usually didn't bother her, but today she hunched behind the wheel, flinching when huge trucks blew by and crazy drivers darted in front of her.

The airport sign loomed ahead, and Savannah took the exit with a whooshing breath of relief. Now she needed to find the remote lot, park, and take a shuttle to the terminal. Then the first leg of the journey would be over.

After triple-checking her bags to make sure she had everything she needed, Savannah waited for the shuttle. The day was warming nicely, the sun shining in an almost cloudless sky. The light breeze carried a hint of salt from the ocean a short distance away.

Suddenly exhausted, Savannah shut her eyes, soaking in the sun's warmth. She didn't even hear the shuttle pull up.

A soft female voice called out, "You coming or going?"

Savannah startled out of her daze, seeing that the shuttle driver was patiently waiting. "Oh, I'm going." She hurried toward the shuttle and hopped aboard. "Sorry."

"That's fine," the driver said. "We all could use a little more sleep around here." She gave a huge, exaggerated yawn. "I've been up since four."

The other passengers chimed in with agreement and laughter.

Cheered by the banter, Savannah found a seat. As she settled in for the ride, she pulled up the weather. Uh-oh, she was heading into fifty degrees and rain. She was glad she'd packed a raincoat.

At the terminal, Savannah got off the shuttle. After going through security, she would find a restaurant and eat breakfast. But first she needed to take a couple of pictures. She stood near a departure sign and snapped a selfie.

Before she could post it online, a little boy crying nearby distracted her. "I can't find Mooey."

His mother hunkered down beside him. "I'm sorry, but we need to get in line. We don't want to miss our flight."

Glistening tears trailed down the boy's cheeks. "You mean Mooey will have to stay behind?" He tugged at her sleeve. "No, Mommy. She'll be scared."

Savannah's heart went out to the child. At his age, a special toy meant the world. "Can I help you look?" she asked.

His mother's shoulders sagged. "Thank you. Maybe we'll be able to find it. It's a stuffed black-and-white cow. It's his favorite." She fished for a tissue in her fleece jacket pocket and wiped the boy's face.

Savannah had guessed as much by the name. "All right. When did you last see Mooey?"

The mother tapped a finger on her lips. "We had it when we got off the shuttle. I remember that. But then I stopped to check a bag outside. And we also got boarding passes printed at the kiosks over there."

"Let me search outside." Still carting her carry-on and handbag, Savannah trotted to the entrance doors. To her left was curbside check-in, so she went in that direction, scanning the sidewalk for the stray toy.

Two porters were working the station, tagging bags and greeting passengers.

One spotted her approaching. "Can I help you, miss?"

"I hope so. I'm looking for a stuffed cow. A little boy seems to have misplaced it." Savannah spotted a trash can and paused to peek inside in case someone had thrown Mooey away. Paper cups, food wrappers, and newspapers were the only things she could see. She didn't want to start digging.

"I haven't seen it. Let me ask Joe." The porter waited until his fellow employee finished hefting huge suitcases onto a conveyor belt. "Hey, Joe, you find a stuffed animal?"

"A cow," Savannah clarified, leaving the trash can for the moment.

"Is this it?" Joe reached behind the counter and pulled out a cow. He gave Savannah a funny look when she made an exclamation of joy and rushed forward, hand outstretched.

"It's not mine," Savannah explained. "Mooey belongs to a little boy inside the terminal. And you have just made his day." She tucked the stuffed animal under her arm.

"Mooey, huh?" Joe pushed back his cap, then settled it more firmly on his head. "Well, have a good day."

"Glad we could help," the other porter added.

"Me too. Thanks." Savannah's response was heartfelt. She waved goodbye to the porters and waited for a couple of cars to pass before going back across the pedestrian walk.

Mother and child were waiting inside, and when they saw Savannah holding Mooey, their faces lit up in identical expressions of joy and relief.

The boy ran forward, reaching for the toy, and Savannah handed it over. He hugged the cow tightly.

"Thank you so much," the mother said. She glanced at the wall clock. "We'd better get in line. It was nice meeting you."

"Same here," Savannah said, watching the boy cuddle Mooey. He put the toy up to his face and touched noses. Cows had really soft noses, she remembered with a pang. "Have a great trip."

"You too," the mother said. "We're flying to New York. How about you?"

It was on the tip of Savannah's tongue to say, "Me too," but something made her hesitate. Instead, she heard herself say, "I was on my way to New York, but I've changed my mind."

The mother regarded her with confusion. "Well, whatever you decide, have a great day." She steered her son toward the security line with a hand on his shoulder.

"I will," Savannah whispered. A rush of elation made her spirits soar as she turned and hurried for the exit.

She was going back to Magnolia Harbor. If the job in New York was right, it could wait. She needed to be with her family and fulfill her obligations to them first.

Her heart skipped a beat. *And see Logan.*

By some oddity of timing, she got the same shuttle driver again.

The driver regarded her with disbelief when Savannah boarded. "I guess you answered wrong the first time," she said.

Savannah smiled. "Yes, I sure did."

25

Grace

"Good morning," Winnie said as she walked through the inn's front door.

Grace glanced up from behind the reception desk and set aside the note she was holding. "You're early today."

"What can I say?" her aunt replied, shrugging off her jacket. "The older I get, the less I seem to sleep. Gus is already headed to the Halstead place." She hung her jacket on a peg behind the counter. "They're making a big push today."

"That's what I heard," Grace said. "Dylan and Phillip already went over too."

"How's everything here?" Winnie asked.

"Savannah left this morning. I found her key and a note on the counter." Grace put the key that accompanied the note back in its place.

Winnie's expression was alarmed. "Really? But her grandmother's will said they all needed to stay the whole time." She thrust out her bottom lip. "I hope she isn't making a huge mistake."

"Savannah has a job interview in New York," Grace said. "She might appear flighty at times, but I believe she's got a good head on her shoulders."

"I think you're right," Winnie said.

Grace straightened a few papers behind the desk. "Do you want coffee?" She was ready for a second cup, and Charlotte had promised to make her a mushroom omelet with whole-grain toast.

"Do I ever," Winnie replied. "Then let's talk about shelving.

I have some ideas for the pantry and closets. I think Kelli and Etta will love them."

"Sounds good," Grace said as they walked to the kitchen.

Charlotte greeted her aunt. "Would you like an omelet?"

Winnie went straight for the coffeepot and poured a mug of coffee. "No thanks. I had bacon and eggs with Gus already. But I won't say no to another slice of toast."

"We'll have one fewer for breakfast," Grace told Charlotte. "It looks like Savannah already checked out."

Charlotte deftly sliced mushrooms. "So we only have Abel and Amy. They must be sleeping in, because I haven't seen them yet."

As if on cue, Abel poked his head into the kitchen. "Sorry to interrupt."

Charlotte gestured him in. "Not at all. How can we help you?"

Abel entered the kitchen. "I'd like to take my wife breakfast in bed. Would that be possible?" He clasped his hands in front of him, earnest entreaty on his handsome features.

"Of course it would," Charlotte said. "We have a whole bunch of trays just for that purpose. What would you like?"

Grace sat on a stool beside Winnie. "Should we check out those shelves?" she said in a soft voice, leaving Charlotte and Abel to their discussion of breakfast.

"Sure." Winnie pulled her phone out of her pocket. "I have some photos to show you." She set the phone on the counter between them and scrolled through the pictures with her index finger.

Abel was now helping Charlotte prepare the tray. He poured mugs of coffee and added fixings, along with silverware and napkins. Charlotte filled two bowls with oatmeal and added fruit.

By the time Abel left with the room service meal, Grace had chosen the pantry configuration she liked best. "We need to get

Charlotte's opinion too," she said. "Since she actually has a pantry she uses daily."

Charlotte heated an omelet pan. "I'd love to take a peek." She threw a teasing glance over her shoulder. "I might get some ideas to revamp mine."

"Anything you want, sister of mine," Grace said. "As long as you keep this great food coming." Grace liked to cook, but she had to admit that she was spoiled having a chef for a sister, especially one who lived at the same address.

Winnie moved on to bedroom closets, and she and Grace conferred about those choices.

"I love all the options," Grace said. "I remember when a closet had only one rod and a jumble of shoes on the floor."

"Yeah, I remember that closet," Charlotte said. "From when I used to borrow your clothes."

Grace laughed at the memory. "She did, the little scamp."

"That's what sisters are for," Winnie said with complacency. "I used to do the same thing to your mother."

Charlotte soon set a plate in front of Grace. The thick omelet was oozing with melted cheese and studded with mushrooms and onions. She put a smaller plate in front of Winnie. It held a slice of the same whole-grain toast she'd given Grace. A tray of jellies was the last item she provided, since napkins and salt and pepper were already on the counter.

As Grace and Winnie enjoyed their delicious food, Charlotte commented on Abel's thoughtful gesture. "I'm sure Amy will be pleased with breakfast in bed."

"It's amazing what giving up your phone for a few days can do," Grace said.

Winnie's smile held satisfaction. "Dorothy Prescott was a very wise woman."

Grace agreed, but it was too bad her youngest granddaughter had cut and run. When people were young, impulsive decisions were easy to make. At a later age, the pros and cons were often more thoroughly weighed.

Grace hoped Savannah had made the right choice.

26

Amy

Amy slept later and more deeply than she had in years. When she finally opened her eyes, sunlight edged the curtains. Rolling over, she stretched out a hand but found only empty space.

Shock made her sit up. Where was Abel? Did she dream that he'd returned and they had reconciled last night? That they had talked for hours, sharing confidences and dreams? Amy sat with her knees up, chewing on a fingernail and racking her brain.

Fumbling sounded at the room door, and a couple of seconds later it opened to reveal Abel, carrying a tray.

An inquisitive Winston was right behind him. The little dog slipped between Abel's legs and hopped up onto the bed to greet Amy.

She laughed and patted the dog. "I was wondering where you went," she said to Abel. Her pounding heart settled into a more normal rhythm.

Abel set the tray on the dresser. "I brought you breakfast in bed." He ferried over a cup of coffee first, knowing that she needed a boost of caffeine before anything else.

"Thank you." Amy blew on the hot liquid and sipped. "I can't believe I slept so late."

Seeing that she was busy, Winston jumped down and began to explore the room.

"Me neither," Abel said, grinning. He carried over a bowl of oatmeal and a tiny pitcher of almond milk.

Amy set the mug on the bedside table and picked up the bowl.

Charlotte had topped the oatmeal with strawberries and blueberries. She took a couple of bites. "It tastes great."

He sat in a chair with his own bowl of oatmeal, a cup of coffee close to hand. "I agree," he said after eating a spoonful of oatmeal.

Winston came and sat at his feet, gazing up hopefully.

"I'm sorry, Winston," Abel said. "But this isn't for you."

The dog made a grunt of dismay, then plopped down and rested his head on his paws.

Amy laughed. "He's such a character." They'd never had time for a pet. Maybe now that they were both going to work from home, at least part of the time, they could finally get one. "I wouldn't mind having a dog like Winston."

Hearing his name, the dog pricked up his ears, earning another laugh from the couple.

"A dog would be great," Abel said, studying his oatmeal. "But I was kind of thinking of a different addition to the family."

At first she didn't get it. "You mean a cat?" she said. Then she saw the tide of red creeping up his neck. "Oh, Abel." Her heart twisted with an almost painful joy and longing. He was talking about having a baby. Tears pooled in her eyes. "I'd love that too."

Abel set the bowl of oatmeal down and walked over to the bed. He bent and kissed Amy. "I love you." Then he returned to his seat. "Okay, now that's settled, what's the agenda for today?"

The beautiful fall weather had brought out visitors in droves, and downtown Magnolia Harbor was hopping.

Amy and Abel parked on a side street, and they walked hand in hand down to the waterfront. The mood was lively, helped along by music from the bandstand and the laughter of children at the playground.

"So what are we doing?" Abel asked when they reached the booths.

"I'm going to introduce you to the potters I want to represent," Amy said. "I want your opinion on the pieces I picked out."

He jabbed a thumb at his chest. "My opinion? Why? I don't know anything about pottery."

"I don't either. But I don't want to rely only on my own taste. People buy things I think are ugly all the time." She turned to a booth, where several people were browsing, and motioned toward a display of mugs, each one more hideous than the last. They featured faces with marble eyes and white squares for front teeth. "Like those."

Abel rubbed his chin, his elbow cupped in his hand. "I think they're hilarious." He pointed. "I especially like the one with buck teeth and crossed eyes."

Amy sighed. "See? That's a perfect example. Let's go talk to the artists."

After strolling through the booths and chatting to the potters, they sat at a picnic table with large glasses of lemonade.

Abel tapped the tabletop. "This is where we sat with Savannah and Logan." He gave her a smug smile. "It seemed to me like a little romance was brewing there."

"I thought so too," Amy said. "But Savannah took off for New York this morning. She got a job interview with a top designer."

"She left before the time was up?" Abel sounded surprised. "That was a bold move. Isn't your inheritance contingent on staying?"

"Yes, that's my understanding." Amy shrugged. "But that's Savannah. I love her dearly, but she's impulsive. Don't get me wrong. She works hard at her profession. Even if I don't really understand it." Actually, she thought it was extremely frivolous.

Abel lifted his paper cup. "She promotes people's products, which is pretty normal, except she happens to wear them." He took a long sip.

His offhand comment struck a chord in Amy. "That's true. I have to admit she's gifted at getting people excited about buying new things. That's why the designer is interested in hiring her."

"You should hire her to help you market the pottery." Abel grinned. "Why should strangers benefit from your sister's genius?"

"You are so right. How great would it be if we could start our own family business?" Amy pulled out her phone, which Winnie had given back permanently, and sent her sister a text. "It's probably too late, but it's worth a shot."

27

Savannah

The return trip to Magnolia Harbor seemed to fly by. Savannah opened the sunroof, cranked up the radio, and even sang along to her favorite hits. Thank goodness no one was around to listen to her off-key singing. With every mile, she felt more lighthearted, more certain that her impulsive decision was the right one.

The Scripture Grammie had given her came to mind during the weather report. *Turn away my eyes from looking at worthless things, And revive me in Your way.*

Well, she certainly felt revived, full of new energy and excitement.

A text came in, but Savannah didn't read it, wanting to obey the law about phone use while driving. Once she pulled off the exit, she drove the familiar route to the farm. She needed to check on Annabelle.

And see Logan, of course. Her heart thumped.

Gladys was setting a crate of apples on the table outside the farm stand. When she spotted Savannah, she lifted a hand and waved.

Savannah pulled up in front of the booth and rolled down her window.

"I thought you had flown the coop," Gladys said with a laugh. "Glad to see you're back."

"I made it all the way to the airport," Savannah admitted. "But then I realized something. I didn't want to go to New York." She glanced up at the deep blue sky. "I love this place too much."

Gladys chuckled. "Don't we all?" She picked up an apple and held it out to Savannah. "Fresh off the tree this morning."

Savannah took a crunching, sweet bite. "It's delicious."

"The men are in the barn, if you're wondering," Gladys said with a teasing smirk. She rearranged the fruit to better effect. "I hope you're staying for lunch."

"I will, if you'll have me." Waving the apple, Savannah pulled ahead and turned into the farm drive. She parked in her usual spot, next to Logan's truck. She climbed out and started walking toward the barn, but then she noticed her shoes were totally inappropriate. So she returned to the car and changed into her rubber boots. Her outfit would be okay, unless they wanted her to work. Then she'd change.

In the barn doorway, she rapped her knuckles on the frame. "Knock, knock."

"Who's there?" Roy called from somewhere inside the barn. A moment later, he stuck his head out around a stall wall. He did a double take. "Is that really you?" He gestured. "Come on down."

Once he disappeared behind the wall, Savannah heard Logan say, "Who was it? Anyone I know?"

"I think you might," Roy said.

Savannah picked up the pace, eager to put him out of his suspense. By the time she reached the stall, she was breathless from moving the heavy, clunky boots. "Hi, guys."

Logan, who was hunkered down beside Annabelle and Maisie, stared up at her in confusion. "I thought you were going to New York."

"I was, but I changed my mind." She kicked at a clump of hay. "Guess I prefer this to the Big Apple. Pretty crazy, huh?"

Roy regarded her with something that looked like approval. "I think you made the right choice, but what does an old farmer know?" He clapped Logan on the back. "I'm going to the house. I think you can take it from here."

"But I thought we—" Logan stopped as Roy's meaning obviously sank in. "Oh. See you in a bit." He rose as Roy waved and disappeared. He peered at Savannah. "I'm thrilled you're here. But are you sure about this? That was a big interview."

At first, Savannah was a tiny bit hurt that he hadn't swept her into his arms, although they hadn't actually gotten that far in their relationship. But she had to admit she understood his reservation. What if she changed her mind tomorrow and took off, leaving him in the lurch? That wouldn't be fair.

"Yes, I am," she said simply, her hand resting on her heart. "I've been pushing and striving and working to get a call like that from a designer for so long. But along the way, my dream changed, and I didn't realize it until I almost left."

"How did your dream change?" he asked.

Savannah patted Annabelle on the head, receiving a lick from the little calf in return. "Working here is so much more real, and I'm with people I care about. My fashion job is all on the surface, including the relationships." Then she smiled, brandishing her apple core. "Plus, the fresh food is great."

Logan stepped forward, his hand moving to cup her chin. "I'm so glad you're back." He gave her a light kiss.

"Me too," she said, her mouth still close to his. Then her belly rumbled, making them both laugh. "What time is lunch?"

28

Grace

Grace watched Charlotte whip up a batch of cookies while chatting with her and Winnie about the brisket judging to be held that night at the festival.

The front doorbell chimed, interrupting their conversation.

"I'll go see who it is," Grace offered and hurried to the foyer. Usually guests walked inside, but no one was waiting for her at the reception desk. Grace went to the door.

An older, attractive woman stood on the front porch. She was dressed in a tailored lilac pantsuit with a silk shirt underneath. Her few pieces of jewelry were gold and tasteful. On the drive behind her sat a gleaming silver Mercedes sedan. Amy and Abel's car was gone, Grace noticed fleetingly. They must have slipped out and gone somewhere.

"Welcome to the Magnolia Harbor Inn," Grace said. The woman looked vaguely familiar, but she couldn't place where she had seen her. "How may I help you?"

"You must be Grace Porter." The woman extended a slender hand. "I'm Dorothy Prescott."

A swooning feeling came over Grace, and she had to grab the doorjamb for support. "Sorry," she said, shaking the woman's hand. "I thought you said Dorothy Prescott."

The woman's handshake was firm and assertive. "I did. I believe you have my grandchildren in residence. And my attorney too."

Grace tried to swallow, but her throat was bone-dry. She coughed. "I'm sorry. Please do come in." She stood back to let Dorothy enter, taking the opportunity to lean on the doorjamb. Her mind was swirling with shock and confusion. She'd thought Dorothy had passed away. But here she was, alive and in very good health, if the sparkle in her pale-blue eyes and the grip of her handshake were anything to go by.

Dorothy threw her an amused glance. "My apologies for barging in on you like this." She put a hand on Grace's arm. "And please do forgive me for the subterfuge. But I needed to do something drastic to put those kids on the right track."

"It's okay," Grace said, but inwardly she was wondering how the siblings would feel once they learned they'd been staying here under false pretenses. Dorothy had used their innate greed to get them to comply.

A sad expression crossed Dorothy's face. "I know a lot of the blame can be laid at my feet. I was far too indulgent and too busy to pay them enough attention when they were younger."

Not knowing how to respond, Grace asked, "Would you like coffee? Tea? Something to eat? We have blueberry muffins. Or my sister can make you a sandwich."

"I'd love a cup of coffee and a muffin," Dorothy said. "Please don't put yourself out."

Grace decided to take her into the kitchen to meet Charlotte and Winnie. The atmosphere was more informal and relaxed there than in the dining room. "Follow me," she said.

Before they left the foyer, a small bundle of brown lightning came bolting down the stairs, claws scrabbling for purchase on the polished floors.

"Oh my," Dorothy said. "Who is this little fellow?"

"That's Winston." Grace had been wondering where the dog had been hiding. Sometimes he liked to go up and spend time with the guests, then take a snooze in a sunny window in the hallway.

Dorothy bent to pat him, cooing endearments.

Winston fell in love and trailed them to the kitchen.

In the doorway, Grace cleared her throat. When Winnie and Charlotte looked up, she said, "Dorothy Prescott has joined us."

Both reeled in shock, but they managed to control any outbursts as Grace made the introductions.

"It's so nice to meet you," Winnie said. "Your grandchildren are delightful. And of course, everyone in Magnolia Harbor loves the arts center and the pottery festival."

Dorothy's cheeks pinked. "That's nice of you to say. I didn't want them to put my name on the building, but they insisted."

Grace filled a mug with coffee, slid a muffin onto a small plate, and gave them to their unexpected guest.

Dorothy accepted them with thanks, then glanced around. "So where are my heirs?" She said the last word with a humorous inflection.

Grace exchanged glances with Charlotte. "Dylan and Amy, along with Abel, are carrying out their assignments. But I'm afraid Savannah checked out this morning."

The older woman bit her lip. "Oh dear. Where did she go?"

"New York," Grace said. "Her note said she has a job interview there."

Dorothy focused her gaze on her mug. "She is so caught up in that fashion business. I was hoping . . ."

Grace didn't press her to elaborate. Instead, she said, "We do have a room available. In fact, you paid for it. Shall I show it to you after you're done with your snack?"

"That sounds fine," Dorothy said. "I'd like to rest before I see Amy and Dylan." She took a bite of muffin, expressing appreciation.

The conversation turned to other topics. Dorothy asked thoughtful questions of all three, showing a sincere but gentle interest. Charlotte mentioned the brisket contest, and it was decided that everyone would go down to the park for dinner.

As they chatted, Grace decided that Dorothy was quite a woman. She was intelligent, charming, and a philanthropist.

But her stomach tightened with anticipation when she thought about the upcoming family reunion.

First to return to the inn were Dylan and Phillip, both dirty and exhausted after doing construction all day.

Grace greeted them from behind the front desk, where she'd been filing while she waited for the siblings to arrive. Earlier she had hidden Dorothy's car behind the barn since they would recognize it.

"I'm heading straight up for a shower." Dylan grinned. "And maybe a nap. Tabitha and I are going to the brisket dinner tonight."

"That's great," Grace said. "I was going to suggest it."

The younger man smiled, then trudged up the stairs.

Phillip leaned an elbow on the counter. "I haven't worked that hard since college. But I enjoyed it." He straightened. "I suppose I'd better go get cleaned up. Julep and I are attending the brisket dinner together."

"That's nice," Grace said. "She's a wonderful woman."

"She is," he agreed. "We plan to keep seeing each other. Never too old for love, right?"

Grace waited until she heard Dylan's door close before saying, "I have news. Dorothy arrived today." She pressed her lips together. "I have a feeling you were expecting her."

Phillip had the grace to look sheepish. "Yes, I was." He put up a hand. "But I was only following her instructions. It certainly wasn't my idea."

Grace accepted that. It wasn't really her business, but she couldn't help but feel that the whole situation was highly irregular. "Anyway, Dorothy would like to meet with Amy and Dylan. She'll be in the music room. Maybe you can help me coordinate?"

"Of course," Phillip said. "But right now, I'm going to hop into the shower. I'm not fit to be in the company of man or beast."

A few minutes after he went upstairs, Amy and Abel walked through the door.

"Phillip would like to speak to you both," Grace said. "Please call his room once you're settled."

They agreed, and Grace returned to her filing. At least she could get something done while waiting, and it was a task that didn't require too much thought.

As arranged, Dorothy came downstairs first, wearing a fresh outfit and makeup. After she reached the foyer, she crossed to the desk. "Thank you again for doing this. In the future, I hope we'll spend many more nights in your charming inn."

"We'd like that," Grace said. Dorothy had paid for a long stay, and besides the dietary requirements, the guests had been no trouble.

The older woman went into the music room, which opened onto the foyer. She left the door ajar.

Grace's stomach tightened in anticipation even more. This might be the most unusual family reunion she'd ever seen.

29

Amy

"Abel, can you please get that?" Amy called when someone tapped on the suite door. She put the hairbrush down and studied her reflection in the bathroom mirror. She looked happy. Leaning closer, she saw that the pesky worry line between her brows was gone.

Maybe she could market the quit-your-job beauty treatment. Amy laughed and left the bathroom.

Abel was talking to Dylan by the door.

When Dylan saw his sister, he crossed the carpet in a couple of strides and kissed her cheek. "Hey, how are you doing?"

"I'm great," she said, her hand going to her cheek. She wasn't the only one who looked happy. Dylan had a gleam and a bounce in his step she hadn't seen since he was a small boy. "How about you?"

In answer, he reached for his back pocket and pulled out a folded piece of paper.

Amy and Abel exchanged puzzled glances.

Dylan unfolded the paper carefully, then cleared his throat. "I'm going to read you something, but you have to promise not to laugh."

"We won't," Amy said. "Go ahead. We're all ears."

Dylan cocked his head as he studied her. "Yeah, I always thought your ears were kind of big." He grinned at his own joke.

"That's enough," Amy said with a smile. "Get on with it."

"'Assuredly, I say to you, inasmuch as you did it to one of the least of these My brethren, you did it to Me.' That's a Bible verse. Matthew 25:40." Dylan folded the paper again, careful to make the same creases.

"Grammie gave it to me. And I finally figured out what it means."

"She gave me a different verse," Amy said. "It completely changed my perspective on things."

"Mine too." Dylan slid the paper into his pocket. "I realized it when we were helping the Halsteads." He blinked rapidly, and to Amy's amazement, she saw tears. "To think that I looked down on them because they're not millionaires like my usual clients."

"Humbling, isn't it?" Amy said softly. "I had to find a new yardstick for my life as well."

Dylan took a deep breath, making his chest expand. "So, I've decided to set up a new company. I'm going to focus on building attractive, comfortable homes on modest budgets." He set his chin as though anticipating objections.

"That's excellent," Abel said, shaking Dylan's hand. "I know you'll be very successful."

Amy gave her brother a big hug. "I'm so proud of you." She released him and picked up the room phone. "I'm going to call Phillip. Then we're going to celebrate tonight. Your new business and mine."

"Yours?" Dylan asked.

Everything had been such a whirlwind that Amy hadn't had a chance to fill in her brother about her latest plans. She quickly brought him up to speed.

"I'm proud of you too," Dylan said.

When Amy called Phillip, he asked them to meet him in the music room.

The trio went downstairs, where Grace greeted them from behind the front desk.

"Are you going to the dinner in the park tonight?" Amy asked her. "We are." Amy and Abel wouldn't eat brisket, but they'd been assured that vegan options would be available.

"I am," Grace said. "It promises to be a really good time. I'm glad you're going." With a smile, she went back to her paperwork.

"I'm going to miss staying here," Dylan said. "Although I'll be back in town, so maybe I can book some more nights." He grinned. "Tabitha and I are officially dating."

Amy nudged her brother's arm. "Fantastic. She's wonderful."

The door to the music room was ajar, and Amy pushed it open wide as she entered, Abel and Dylan behind her. Phillip and an older woman were seated in armchairs. They both rose to greet them.

At first, Amy couldn't take in what she was seeing. Then the woman in front of her smiled. It was Grammie.

Amy's head swam, and her knees felt weak. "Grammie?" Her voice sounded high-pitched and thin. She was barely aware of Abel behind her, propping her up.

"Yes, it's me," her grandmother said as she stood. "I hope you can forgive me for tricking you this way. But I didn't know how else to get through to you kids." She smiled at her attorney. "And don't blame Phillip. I made him do it."

Dylan pushed past Amy and gathered his grandmother into a hug. "I'm thrilled to see you. Whatever you were thinking, it worked. I have so much to tell you."

Grammie laughed. "And I want to hear it all."

When Dylan stepped aside, Amy hugged her grandmother. She suddenly thought of Savannah's abrupt departure. A knot formed in her stomach at the idea of telling Grammie what happened.

The front door of the inn opened and shut, and Amy heard Savannah talking to Grace. To Amy's relief and joy, her sister was back. She must have changed her mind.

"Are you surprised to see me?" Savannah asked with a laugh. "I'm surprised to be here. But happy."

Her grandmother bustled out of the room. "Is that my little girl?"

Savannah gasped, putting a hand to her mouth. "Grammie, is it really you?"

"It's me," her grandmother said. "Now get over here and give me a hug."

Savannah ran across the floor, and the two women embraced.

Dylan gave Amy a thumbs-up and a wink.

Amy smiled at Abel, then slipped her arm through his. She'd never take her husband or her family for granted again.

"Will you forgive me?" Grammie asked Savannah. "I'm sorry I tricked you all this way, but I didn't know what else to do to shake you up."

Savannah kissed her grandmother's cheek. "Of course I do. I'm just so happy to have you back."

"Did you get my text?" Amy asked Savannah.

"I haven't had a chance to read it yet," Savannah said. "I hope it wasn't urgent."

"Not urgent," Amy assured her sister. "I just want to hire you to help me market local pottery. You'll be perfect."

Savannah's eyes widened. "Really? I'd love that." She pointed at her rubber boots. "I'm also going to work on Logan's farm."

"Who is Logan?" her grandmother asked.

"He's my new . . . friend." Savannah blushed.

"I can't wait to hear about Logan and the farm. And everything else." Grammie put an arm around Savannah's shoulders and smiled. "So, how do you like working with cows?"

30

Grace

"**G**ood turnout," Spencer said to Grace.

They stood under the tents set up for the brisket contest and dinner. A blue dusk was falling over the lake, and hanging lanterns and standing heaters gave the tent a cozy feel. Behind the contestants' table, Charlotte and Dean conferred with the head judge. They would taste the entries and announce winners before the meal got started.

"I'm really glad to see so many people here," Grace said. She knew how much work went into these community events. A thrill ran through her when she thought about the program. A last-minute change had been made that would surprise everyone. She was tempted to tell Spencer, but she decided not to. She wanted him to experience it for himself.

The Halstead family came along the paved path with Dylan and Tabitha. Kelli waved when she spotted Grace and Spencer, and the family changed course to join them.

"How are you doing?" Grace asked Evan.

The boy beamed. "I'm doing great. And guess what? I caught up with all my schoolwork already."

"That's impressive," Spencer said. "You must have been working hard."

"He needs to study," his sister said. "Dylan gave him a new job. Tell them, Evan."

Evan pointed at his chest, his face bright with joy. "I'm the assistant project manager for the new house. I get to give my input. Dylan says the experience will help me when I become an architect."

Grace had no doubt that was true. "That's wonderful, Evan. Congratulations."

Up at the front of the tent, feedback sang out from a microphone held by Missy Perkins. "Sorry about that, folks. We're almost ready to begin the brisket contest, but before that I have a very special announcement. Tonight we're honored to have one of the sponsors of our pottery festival here with us. Everyone, please give Dorothy Prescott a warm welcome."

Spencer raised his brows as he glanced at Grace. "But I thought she had passed?"

Grace laughed. "No, I'm afraid the rumors of her death were greatly exaggerated."

As Grace watched Dorothy and her family enter the tent with a new lightness surrounding all of them, she realized one thing for certain.

The Magnolia Harbor Inn had worked its magic once again.

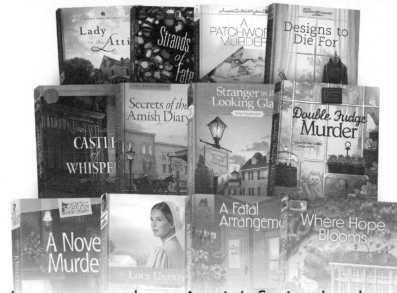